Six Second Slack

I hope you enjoy the book! Best wishes,

Rachel C. Hecta

California Rodeo

Six Second Slack

Rachel Claus Hector

Writers Club Press
San Jose New York Lincoln Shanghai

Six Second Slack

Writers Club Press
an imprint of iUniverse, Inc.

For information address:
iUniverse, Inc.
5220 S. 16th St., Suite 200
Lincoln, NE 68512
www.iuniverse.com

ISBN: 0-595-21513-0

Printed in the United States of America

For everyone at Indian Springs Ranch.
Without you this book would not have been possible.
For Chiquita.

Acknowledgements

I would like to thank all my friends who helped me with the book, whether they know it or not, my parents, my sister, and all the country singers who inspired the musical portions of this book.

CHAPTER 1

"Come on, girl. That's it." Alyson soothed the bay Arabian mare as she came pounding down the ramp. The noise of the truck and the sound of her feet on the flimsy wooden ramp must have scared Chiquita all the way from Washington State to Wherever-This-Was, California.

The bay's nostrils flared, showing their deep pink insides as she picked her way backwards down the ramp. Her coat was plastered with sweat underneath the shipping blanket and her head was held as high as Alyson's grip on the lead would allow it.

"Easy, just take it slow," she instructed the mare, trying to stay calm herself. Chiquita lowered her head and snorted before backing off the ramp much too quickly. As soon as the mare was on the ground, she snapped her head up high again and let out a whinny that carried through the whole stable.

Alyson smiled at the mare's antics and studied the surroundings. They were in a courtyard bordered on one side by a towering barn that looked new. The stable seemed so modern next to the surrounding countryside. Each stall not only had an inside area, but a yard just as big behind it. At her old stable, the barn had been wooden and the stalls just boxes. This would definitely be an improvement, right? She wasn't so sure.

Chiquita danced around her, showing off her Arabian spirit. When Alyson scolded her gently she stopped and stood still for a few moments. As Alyson's mother talked with a woman, presumably the stable manager, she looked around again. No one else was near, but there were more horses than she'd ever seen in one place. A barbed wire fenced pasture that must have been at least fifty acres bordered one side of the courtyard. On the other side of the barn was an arena, and behind it more small paddocks. Apparently this place had a lot of boarders, which struck her as strange since the areas that they had driven through as they followed the hired horse trailer seemed incredibly isolated. At least she might find someone her own age.

The lady who had been talking to her mother finished speaking and approached Alyson. She smiled and extended her hand, "You must be Alyson. I'm Carole, the barn manager."

Alyson nodded and returned Carole's firm grip. Her hands were rough and her face was weathered, but she had a bright smile and clear blue eyes. She wore her brown hair cropped short.

Behind Alyson, Chiquita jumped as a tractor pulled out into the pasture. The large machine had a trailer filled with hay attached to it as. it rumbled over the hard and bumpy ground. The mare stood watching it for a long time, shuddering.

"It's all right, old girl," Carole said softly and offered her hand for the bay to sniff. Turning to Alyson, she added, "It takes a while for some horses to get used to the noise. Most of them realize soon enough that it means food is on the way. But, anyway, I have to meet someone in town in about a half hour, so I'll show you the stall she'll be in."

Alyson nodded again and realized she hadn't yet said anything. She forced a smile. "That would be great."

They proceeded up the slight hill into the barn, so obviously new with its fireproof metal and plastic construction. Twelve stalls lined each side of a pristine cement aisle. The doors were the type that slid open, and the top half of the walls of the stall were made of metal bars.

As the mare stepped onto the cement floor, she snorted loudly, blowing through her nostrils. Alyson let her sniff it for a second before they continued, the bay picking her feet up high, as though she were walking through knee deep mud. Carole stopped when the foursome reached a stall about halfway down,.

"*Voilà*. You can put any trunks here," she gestured, "and everything else should be ready. She gets two bags of bedding per month.," She pointed again to two full bags of shavings lying near the stall, ", Although you can always buy more. I hope I'm not being too quick here, but I do have to go. Overbooked."

"No," Alyson said shyly, "no, that's fine."

"Thank you for seeing us in," Alyson's mother said. She and Carole passed Allyson and the mare on their way to the office at the end of the barn.

Just as they reached the end of the aisle, she turned and called, "Aly, I'm going. I'll pick you up in a few hours. Have fun!"

Alyson smiled weakly at her mother and turned her attention back to Chiquita, who was inspecting the bags of bedding for something edible. She tethered the mare loosely to the bars of the stall, slid open the door, and inspected its inside. Its spaciousness seemed even larger with the yard. The floor was well outfitted with rubber mats, which would be even more comfortable with bedding on them. The stall was definitely the nicest Chiquita would ever occupy.

She stepped outside to undo the mare's blanket and put her shipping boots away before realizing that her tack trunk had not yet arrived. Hadn't Carole mentioned something earlier about the stable help bringing it from the truck, along with all of her tack?

"Oh, well. Might as well just get her settled." Alyson would rather have taken the trunk out herself, but it was too heavy. And she had Chiquita to deal with. Her mother was content to let the hired help do what they were paid for, but Alyson thought this would come off sort of snobbishly to the people at the stable.

She loosened the knot on the bars, pulled the rope up and circled it in a noose around the bay's neck. But before she knew it, Chiquita had found something that didn't suit her and spooked. She jumped away, the rope sliding through Alyson's hands, and took off at a gallop out of the barn.

Hastily, Alyson grabbed the end of the mare's tail in an attempt to stop her, but Chiquita just flicked one of her hind legs at her and continued in a mad dash for the door. She swerved out of hoof's way and ran after the distraught mare. She couldn't let her trip on the rope and hurt herself, or run up the road they'd come and escape into the chaparral outside the stable. Plus, Chiquita was still outfitted in a blanket and shipping boots.

But as they reached the end of the aisle, Alyson realized that there was a building in front of them across the dirt road that brought them here. If the mare decided to turn left, she would run toward an arena much larger than the first one she'd seen, and a barn made of pipe corral fencing. Beyond that, all she would hit would be more small paddocks and the border of the large pasture. If she decided to turn right, she could escape onto the road.

Thankfully, Chiquita decided that left was the best choice, and Alyson's heart fell from her throat back into its normal place. She slowed to catch her breath, knowing the bay would eventually stop. The trouble was making sure she did so off of the entrance road. After Alyson rested for a split second, she continued in pursuit of her horse.

To her relief, three people stood around the corner of the pipe barn holding the bay mare—two guys and a girl. The horse was prancing on her tiptoes and her nostrils were flared, but the threesome seemed to have her under control.

Although Chiquita was excited from the run, she stood still for them. The girl had already reached down and pulled off the boots, checking Chiquita's legs to see if they were hot and injured. Alyson was relieved. Obviously these people knew what they were doing.

Alyson's initial relief was replaced by dismay when she realized these people were probably around fifteen or sixteen; she had just turned fifteen. Sure, her *intention* had been to meet people, but how embarrassing! She couldn't even control her own horse and now they were probably going to give her a hard time. They must have already thought she was a total idiot.

"Great," she muttered under her breath and proceeded calmly towards them, eyes down on the dusty ground.

As she reached the trio, Alyson looked up slowly and said shakily, "I'm so...so sorry. She just spooked and..." Before she could go off into a long and drawn out explanation the girl stopped her with a smile.

"No sweat." Her smile was sweet and her face soft, accented by bright blue eyes and golden hair that shone in the summer sun. It was the kind of hair that would look perfect even unbrushed. She looked so perfect in jeans and an ocean blue shirt, that if it hadn't been for her bubbly and somewhat flirtatious personality, Alyson would have figured her for a snob. "She's really sweet, what's her name?"

The girl handed the mare's rope back to her, still smiling. Alyson curled up the corners of her mouth in a shy smile and answered, twisting her hand underneath the shipping blanket to feel how hot the mare was, "Chiquita."

"Like the banana, you mean?" joked one of the guys. He seemed older than Alyson and wore a cowboy hat over his mop of brown hair. His deep brown eyes belied a contagious lopsided smile.

"Yeah, I guess," she said meekly.

The other girl smacked him playfully said, "Ignore him; I always do. Anyway, I'm Catherine, but everyone calls me Cat. This is Sam." She gestured towards the one who had made the joke and then turned to her other side where a boy (also in a cowboy hat) that looked about her age stood. "And this is Mark. Welcome to Indian River Ranch."

"Thanks..." She wasn't quite sure what to say. Cat was very outgoing and at that moment, even though the girl had been nice, all Alyson wanted to do was to go and hide her head underneath Chiquita's mane. "I'm Alyson."

"Well, then, welcome, Alyson." Sam offered his hand formally and she shook it with a grin.

An uncomfortable silence covered them for a moment, so Alyson said, "I guess I'd better go cool her out. It was nice to meet you."

"Whoa, you aren't going to get off that easily." Cat informed her before she could walk away.

"Not with her at least," Mark muttered sarcastically.

She glared at him and turned back to Alyson, saying, "We'll help get you settled."

"Yeah, we don't have much else to do. And either way, Cat won't let us get out of this." This time the comment came from Sam, and the girl tossed a black stare at him, too.

Alyson laughed and said, "All right, thanks." She turned the mare around and set off at a walk. Sam fell into step next to her, Mark on the other side of Chiquita and Cat opposite Sam.

"You'll get used to her after a while," he whispered to her, leaning close so that Cat wouldn't hear. She could almost feel his smile creeping up on her and that made her grin.

"I'm sure," Alyson responded easily, finding it simple to keep up the conversation.

She had a feeling they were going to be friends—not the same as the friends she'd had in Washington, but friends just the same. And the best thing was that the new house was just a little ways up the street. This was Podunk, USA, but maybe that wouldn't matter. There would surely be some schooling shows and excellent trails to ride. And she hadn't yet been to town, but she knew there would at the least be a good tack shop.

"What are you telling her?" Cat asked as they entered the barn. The light was so dim Alyson's eyes had a hard time adjusting.

"Nothing, nothing," Sam said innocently as he tossed Alyson a grin.

They were all laughing by the time they reached the stall. Her now half set up tack trunk was lying open, its brushes strewn across the floor. Hoof polish had spilled all over Chiquita's rolled up polo wraps and her saddle sat against the stall's sliding door.

"Whoa…" Cat started as soon as she saw the black dressage saddle Alyson had saved up all her money to buy. "Dressage?"

"Yeah," Alyson answered as though nothing was wrong. In Washington most of the people at the stable had ridden English style and had either jumped or shown in dressage or pleasure.

"Don't get me wrong, that's cool and all, but you won't find anyone here who rides English," she said, glancing at the saddle again as though it had a plague she didn't want to catch.

"Yeah," Mark added, looking as though he were shocked. "We all do rodeo and stuff like that."

"Like roping." Sam raised his hand as he added this.

"And barrel racing,"

"And penning and stuff," Mark said.

"Well…" Alyson had to fish hard for what she wanted to say. "Chiquita doesn't know anything but dressage." She began walking Chiquita forward after she had dumped her shipping boots into the messy pile.

"She's an Arab, right?" Sam asked to her surprise. Arabs were quite easily identified by their dished faces, and she didn't think he was that stupid. He was just checking—and with a slightly amused tone.

"Yeah. I got her in Washington. She's a Ben Rabba daughter." Alyson rubbed the mare's neck soothingly as she explained Chiquita's bloodlines, which were deeply set in a prestigious line of the English type of the breed.

"She could learn." He seemed to have ignored what she'd added about bloodlines as they left the barn. Although Chiquita's breathing had returned to normal, she was still hot and needed to be cooled out. "I mean, Arabs aren't exactly popular horses for it—you'd get laughed out of Texas if you tried to ride one there—but they have good legs and feet."

"Learn what?" Alyson asked, surprised.

"Well, rodeo. You certainly won't get far here with dressage. The closest dressage shows, or whatever you call them, will be miles from here," he told her frankly. Cat nodded in agreement.

"Yeah, and there are no dressage instructors here," she added, resting her hand on Chiquita's neck.

Alyson's heart sunk. This really *was* Podunk USA. This wasn't just a small town surrounded mostly by farms, but it was also without dressage. She and Chiquita had just become in tune with each other. On every ride they'd had lately Chiquita had been supple and was bending well. They had mastered flying changes, leg yields, and a killer extended trot. Now she was eager to try her hand at a schooling show. "None?" She knew she would die.

"I know all the horse people in this area. This place is all 4-H and agriculture. That means one thing: rodeo. You'll get used to it."

"I have a saddle that would probably fit her," Sam offered, "and you can use it."

"Yeah, and I have a bridle that might fit," Mark added, sizing the mare's head up as he talked.

"But I've never done anything like this before. No offense to you and all, but I don't think we can do this." She was amazed that these three had barely met her and were just about giving their tack to her. The people at her stable in Washington had been nice, but they were nice in a way that was much different.

Chiquita saw the tractor with the hay on it again and stopped, ears pricked forward as the machine rattled along.

"It's okay, big girl." Alyson soothed the mare. After a few more moments, Chiquita lowered her head and was content to follow them along the side of the arena.

"Of course you can do it." This comment came from Sam and was followed by a grin. "I'm sure you could do anything you set your mind to."

"Yo, Sam. Not so deep. You're going to scare her off," Mark said jokingly.

Cat rolled her eyes at the both of them and turned to Alyson., "As I said, ignore them. Anyway, think about the riding thing."

"I will. One question, though: Where are all your horses?"

"I have a Quarter Horse called Buffy," Mark put in with slight trepidation.

"Buffy?" She let the question slip from her mouth, surprised by the name, hoping a second later that she hadn't sounded rude. Seeing as this was a guy's horse, she expected the name to be much more masculine.

"Yeah, she was my sister's before she went off to college," he explained meekly.

"And I also have a Quarter Horse—Poco," Sam entered, then leaving the conversation for Cat to continue.

"Yeah, and I have an Appy called Buck," Cat said as she toyed with Chiquita's black mane.

"Cool." Alyson was at a loss for words.

Cat changed the subject. "So, where do you live? We all live up here except for Mark. He lives in town. His dad's got most of the row crop land around here." She gestured to the hill near them. A badly paved road that connected to the main road to the town tapered off into smaller dirt roads toward a cluster of five houses. Each of the houses was fairly small although they sat on a plot of land of easily fifteen acres.

Alyson gazed downhill to an area patched with different colors of land. What the heck were row crops?

"First house up there." Alyson pointed with her free hand to the house closest to the stable. She had a hard time believing that Mark lived 'in town', when all they'd passed coming to the house was a small market and a gas station. She smiled, trying very hard to think positively. "You guys should come over sometime."

"So *you're* the one that moved in there. We can all take a ride up there tomorrow or something," Mark suggested.

"Yeah, we moved here because my dad got a job with the big dairy working on computers or something... Wait a second, we can *ride* up there?"

"Of course," Cat answered as though the question were a little stupid. "There are tons of trails around here to ride on."

"Awesome," Alyson said as they reached the pipe barn once again and turned around it to head back to the barn.

After a few more seconds of silence, Sam looked at his watch and sighed. "Sorry guys, gotta go. Mom wanted me to be home, like, twenty minutes ago."

He smiled at Alyson and told her, "Nice to meet you, Alyson. I'll see you tomorrow."

She nodded, weakened by his smile and watched him reach the dirt parking lot. He drove off in his white pickup.

"I wouldn't drool too much over him," Cat warned her jokingly when she saw Alyson's expression. "He's sixteen; plus he's got every girl in school kissing his feet."

"But I wasn't ..." She turned back to Cat and tried to formulate an explanation. It was no use, though. Cat had turned her attention elsewhere.

Chapter 2

"Would you mind telling me why you're so deep in thought?" The night air was still and the sound of frogs from the swampy area surrounding the houses filled their ears. Cat and Sam walked steadily down the road, their steps in tune with each other on the uneven pavement.

"Huh?" he asked, turning his head to her. "I asked you why were you so deep in thought," she repeated. Never had she seen Sam so engrossed in his own mind before. Maybe it was just the excitement of the day, of meeting a new friend, or the upcoming rodeos, but she knew he was much too thoughtful for the beginning of summer. Finals were over a week and a half ago, and now that they were free to do what they wanted until the fall, there wasn't anything to worry about.

"Oh, I dunno. There are a lot of things going on, that's all." The excuse was weak. Cat was the same age as Sam, was going to be a junior in high school with him the next fall, and had known him since before she could walk. There was something on his mind. *Or someone, perhaps.* She knew when he had a crush on someone, and he certainly acted like he did.

Crossing her arms, she told him frankly, "You like her, don't you?"

"Who?" he asked innocently, as if he had no clue what she was talking about.

"You know who I'm talking about. Alyson," Cat said firmly, moving closer to him as they walked. She kept her voice down since the valley echoed.

"What? No way," Sam told her, and he shook his head even though it was too dark to see. "She's not even fifteen yet. Besides, I just met her today."

"She *is* fifteen. She told me after you left. And so what? You're still in love with her. It's so obvious." Cat sighed.

He didn't say anything for a moment and then asked, "All right, so what if I do like her? What then?"

"I'm not telling—just going to keep you wondering for a little while longer." She grinned as they made their way up Alyson's driveway.

"You...you *little*...I'm going to get you!" he mocked, chasing her the rest of the way to the door.

Cat rang the doorbell and listened for Alyson's footsteps racingto the doorway. When the door opened, Alyson greeted them.

"Oh, hi. Come on in." Alyson said, surprised.

"Thanks. Just wanted to make sure that you were settled and see if you needed any help." Sam explained as they walked into the entryway.

"Aly, honey, who is it?" Her mother came around the corner and smiled.

"Just a couple friends. They're going to help me put some stuff away."

"Well, hi." She was still smiling as she said this.

Cat and Sam introduced themselves cordially and waited a few moments before stealing away into Alyson's room.

* * *

Alyson was surprised that her friends showed up at the house that night, but was grateful for the help unpacking. It was much more fun when she didn't have to do it by herself.

"Here." She held up the folding shelf as Sam jumped to help her unfold it. "It's for my model horses," she explained and pointed to a herd of plastic and resin horses that paraded across her desk. They cantered between bubble wrap and trotted between packing peanuts.

"Cool! How many do you have?" Cat asked enthusiastically as they scouted for a place to set up the shelf in the small room. It was not much bigger than Alyson's old room back in Washington, but it was shaped much differently. She couldn't quite picture any of her things in it yet.

"Um, quite a few. Over two hundred." She blushed, hoping she didn't sound like she was bragging. "I used to show them...you know, when I lived in Washington. I was hoping I might find some good shows around here, though."

"Awesome." Cat's eyes lit up as they pulled the shelf into a corner.

"All right, this might sound like an idiotic question, but how do you *show* plastic horses?" Sam asked, motioning to the horses on the desk.

Alyson laughed. "Don't worry. I get that a lot. It's not all that confusing once you get used to the idea. It's basically just like real horses."

She made sure he was listening before she continued. No sense explaining if he wasn't really interested. But it seemed as though he was paying rapt attention to her, so she took a deep breath and started, "There are halter and performance classes. In halter, a horse is judged on how it represents the breed you say it is and on condition. If they're original finish, which is, like, how they are when you buy them in the stores, then they're also sometimes judged on how valuable they are."

"But how can you choose if there are thousands of the same models in circulation?" He seemed intrigued.

Alyson smiled. "They're all different because they're hand painted. Sometimes two of the same horses can look completely different. You could also show it as whatever breed you think it looks like, so two of the same ones might be in different breed classes."

"And performance? I mean, they're plastic."

"Well, I'm getting to that. There is more to halter."

Sam sighed. "Sheesh. I'm beginning to think real horses are easier."

Cat nodded in agreement, clearly muddled by her explanation.

"They are," she explained with a grin. "But there are more than just plastic horses. Artists have taken this into their own hands and produced original sculptures, usually made of resin, and have painted and repositioned the plastic ones. They show in a different division. Now, as for performance, there are just as many classes as you can think of at a real horse show. People make tack and obstacles, and using horses that are in moving positions, they make a diorama of sorts. These are judged on suitability of the horse, if the tack is correct, and if the horse is doing what it's supposed to. Get it?"

"Yeah, um, sure." The expression on his face made them all laugh.

Alyson pulled out a box that held some of her horses. Normally, she wouldn't have let anyone else handle them, but she had a feeling that neither was going to harm anything. "Here. You can help me arrange them on the shelf."

Just as she was reaching down to open the box's flaps, Sam bent over to help her and they hit hands. Embarrassed, she pulled away and blushed, hoping he didn't notice how flustered she was.

"Sorry," he said as Cat jumped in to help them.

Alyson wondered if Cat been right that afternoon. She must have been—you didn't feel flustered when just *anyone* hit your hand, did you? She didn't believe in love at first sight, so she brushed it off. It was just nerves.

* * *

When she arrived at the barn the next morning, Alyson was greeted by the unfamiliar chords of country music blaring from a radio on the bench near the large arena. It was only nine in the morning, but Sam, Cat, and Mark were already there. They were gathered around a plump Quarter Horse gelding when she first saw them. The horse was a dark brown that blended into itself over his body. His mane and tail were darker than his coat, but she wouldn't have described him as a bay.

"Hey! What's up?" Cat greeted her merrily. She was leaning forward over a metal hitching post and stroking the brown's nose while Sam and Mark hosed down its tail. The gelding chewed invisible grass inside his mouth, about to fall asleep. His ears flopped lazily to the sides, almost like a rabbit's.

"Not much since last night." Alyson said as she approached them. "What's up here?"

"Washing old Poco's tail. He lives out in the pasture," Mark threw his head in the direction of the pasture to show her, "and Sam says he gets everything imaginable in his tail, so we volunteered to help clean it out."

"But we'll be done in a sec. Go get your mare. We're going to go for a trail ride," Sam told her, pulling a wet burr out of the gelding's thick black tail.

"You know, I thought, since we've only been here for a day and all that I might just..." But she couldn't finish the pathetic excuse for a sentence because Sam cut her off.

"It'll help her settle in to meet our horses and check out the area."

For some reason, Sam's words convinced her to go on the ride. Normally, when she didn't want to do something, she wouldn't budge. But then again, she reasoned, this was *riding*. Since when did it take convincing to get her on Chiquita's back? *Since this is all so different*, Alyson's mind screamed. She knew it was true—in Washington there had been no risks, nothing different except for new dressage maneuvers. *But hey*, her mind put in again. *It's only a risk if there's something to lose. I have nothing to lose. And either way I'll have to get used to this.*

"Yeah, and we'd better get the horses ready soon if we want to be back before it's really hot," Cat put in, her eyes wandering up to the clear blue sky.

"Go get Chiquita while we finish up here and then we can go find some tack for you." Sam rinsed out Poco's tail one last time, squeezing the water out by running his hands down the course brown hair.

"Yeah," Mark chuckled. "You don't want to look like a dressage rider around here or you'll get run out of the place. Especially on an Arab."

Although she didn't find the words at all funny, Alyson hurried to the barn, calling her mare's name. Chiquita nickered so loudly that the sound echoed throughout the barn. Smiling and rejuvenated by the familiar call, she unhooked the halter from the door handle and slid open the door.

Chiquita lifted her head, excited, and practically dove into the halter as Alyson pulled it up and buckled it. Alyson studied the bay for a few moments; she was lighter than she had been in the winter and her well formed shoulder, hindquarter, and back muscles flexed as she moved. She had a wide white star on her forehead and a lopsided snip dripping down her muzzle. In Alyson's opinion, she was the most beautiful horse in the world, especially with her exotic dished Arabian face. She kissed Chiquita on the nose and ran her hands over her neck, scratching an itchy spot near her shoulder, before leading her out of the stall.

By the time they had walked to the arena, there were two more horses tied near Poco. One was easily the homeliest Appaloosa she'd ever seen; he was fat as a tick and thick buckskin, brown, and frosty white spots flecked his hindquarters. His dark tail didn't reach down more than a foot and his equally dark mane was as tall as the grass on a golfing green. He had an oversized, but strangely cute, head that was a mix of buckskin and frost, and a shag carpet for an underbelly. After a few seconds, she realized that it must have been Buck, Cat's gelding.

The other horse was a sturdy buckskin Quarter Horse mare who stood tethered near Buck. She was thick boned and had a bulldog stature. A dark dorsal stripe looked as though it had been painted down her back and a large white star accented her face. Alyson strained to remember the name she could hear Mark saying in her mind. Was it Fluffy? No, Buffy. That was it.

"Here." Sam's voice startled her from behind and she had to think quickly so as not to startle Chiquita by jumping. "This should fit her," he said as he sized up Chiquita's back with his eyes. He laid the heavy western saddle down on the bench with a *clunk*.

"Uh, thanks," Alyson said, unsure if she was thankful or not. In the pit of her stomach she was still worried. *It wouldn't have mattered if we'd never left Washington*. The angry thought clouded her mind. California was so different, and different usually meant fun and interesting. The Alyson back in Washington would never have turned down a chance to go exploring on horseback. Why should she be worried now? Confused, she pushed the thoughts away.

"No problem." His words snapped her back into reality. "Cat and Mark went searching for a bridle. Here, tether her to the bar on Gabby's stall—the end one—and we can try on the saddle."

Alyson did as she was instructed, moving to the end of the pipe stall and knotting the rope around the metal bar. Patting the chestnut Arabian that occupied the stall, she watched as Sam took the thick saddle pad and placed it on Chiquita's back.

He hoisted the saddle up and laid it down gently on the pad, as though it were a sack filled with feathers. Chiquita turned her head to see what was on her back but didn't protest. She was well trained, an Arabian that could pull carriages and do dressage without spooking unless something surprised her from behind. Normally, which was strange for an Arabian, she was the proverbial bombproof horse.

"Watch carefully. You probably won't get this on the first try, but it helps to watch someone do it." He motioned to the old leather straps of the cinch. As he did them up, Alyson knew he was right about not getting it on the first try. She would be lucky to get it by the tenth try.

"There," Sam announced with a tone of pride when he finished. "I knew this would fit. Angel was just about her size."

"Who?" She couldn't help but ask.

"She was my old horse—a little gray Appaloosa. I had her since she was five. My dad and I started her. Two years ago, when she was nine, she had an accident and had to be put down." He let his words trail.

"Wait a second, why am I telling you this? You don't need to know. Come on, let's go find Mark and Cat. They're bound to have found something good by now."

"No, that's okay," she tried to assure him as they walked back to the barn. Alyson figured they were using the barn as a shortcut to wherever they were going. She had found that it doubled as a walkway even though it was almost easier to walk around it.

All of a sudden, a small dog jumped out into their path and began yapping at them. It looked like nothing more than a ball of orange fur with two beady eyes and four stumps for legs. Its bark was so piercing that Alyson jumped back, startled, and asked, "Oh my gosh, what *is* that?"

Sam, seemingly unperturbed, gathered the little dog in his arms and scratched behind its ears. "This is Tricki Woo. She's Carole's Pomeranian. And she runs the place, so you'd better be careful." He held the now silent dog forward for Alyson to pet.

Tentatively, she presented the little furball her hand. "As in Tricki Woo from the James Herriot books?"

Sam's eyes widened slightly. "I'm surprised you knew. Not many people do."

"Yeah, well, I've read them all." She smiled and rubbed the dog's ears. Tricky turned her head and leaned it into Alyson's fingers as she scratched.

He put the dog gently back on the ground after a few moments. It barked at them as they left, but this time she wasn't fazed. They headed for a clutter of wooden tack rooms that aligned the short side of the small arena across the courtyard. Sam pulled open the door of one and motioned for her to step in ahead of him. They found Cat and Mark kneeling on the floor sorting through a tub of what looked like old leather products.

"Oh, hey." Cat turned to them She held up a bridle for Sam to see. "This was Angel's. Do you think it would work?"

Sam shook his head and joined them. "Chiquita's head is smaller. How about Fawn's old curb?" He asked Mark.

"Oh, yeah. That's back in my box. Let's go get it."

It took them a while to find a bridle that fit Chiquita's strangely shaped head, but they eventually settled on an old copper mouth curb bridle that once belonged to a mare Mark owned when he was younger.

The mare looked strange but somehow good decked out in western tack. The chestnut leather really suited her, although she didn't seem to like the heavier weight on her back. They tightened the cinch one more time and checked that the rest of her tack was in order before gathering in the small open area by the arena.

"So, you wanna go up in the wood?" Sam asked once they had all tacked up and mounted. Poco's ears flopped to the side and he stood with his back leg cocked.

"No," Cat answered, shaking her head vigorously to make her point. "That guy's probably out walking his pig. Buck hates that pig."

Alyson wasn't quite sure she'd heard correctly—since when did people walk *pigs*? California was really twisted. No one she knew and no one she wanted to know walked *pigs*. Besides, the old Appaloosa gelding didn't look like anything bothered him. He actually looked more as though he was ready to fall sleep. She was about to question them about the pig but decided against it.

"How about the frog pond?" Mark suggested. Alyson felt like a fifth wheel spinning without purpose. Her feet felt like they had bricks attached to them in the heavy stirrups, and she wasn't sure exactly how to position herself with the horn of the saddle in the way. She knew she looked like some tourist a pony ride. Even worse, they must all have thought she is a complete idiot. She didn't even feel like she was riding her own horse.

But no one seemed to notice her discomfort. Mark parked Buffy by the bench and bent down to grab the tiny radio. The mare didn't seem to mind that he carried the squawking radio to Sam's pickup and didn't flinch even as it scraped along the truck's bed as it was set down.

"So where exactly are we going?" Alyson worked up the courage to ask. She dropped her feet out of the stirrups and twisted her ankles around. They were sore already.

"The frog pond. It's normally overrun by frogs, which explains the name, but we swim in it sometimes," Cat explained as she pulled Buck up next to Chiquita. The mare laid her ears back at the gelding, but with Alyson on her back she didn't dare do anything more.

"Cool." She tried to let enthusiasm creep into her voice but it was hard, so she just concentrated on the land.

The vegetation on the rolling hills reached the horses' knees and was dotted with all sorts of wild flowers. They climbed slowly and steadily through the golden grass, enjoying the silence. She was thankful she had kept Chiquita in good enough shape to climb.

After a time, the trail gradually reversed its upward slope and turned down. They were forced to cross a dirt track that traced the outline of the roads connecting the houses.

"Watch for cattle. I'm assuming she's never seen them, so I'm just warning you." Mark's words didn't make much sense in her mind.

Yes, cattle. As in *cows*. She knew what they were, but she wasn't quite sure what he meant by 'watch for them'. "What do you mean? Aren't they behind fences?"

Cat looked like she was going to burst out laughing for a moment, but she suppressed her emotion to answer the question. Alyson felt herself turning as red as the burgundy poppies on the shoulder of the road. "Not necessarily. Look. See that grate in the ground?"

She looked where Cat was pointing. Just where the fence opened its jaws to accommodate the road, there was an object on the ground. Actually, it was inlaid in the ground and looked like a set of metal bars spaced less than a foot apart built into the dirt about five feet across.

"What is it?"

"That's a cattle guard," Cat explained. "It would be really annoying if you had to open the gate every time you wanted to drive somewhere, wouldn't it? So what you do is put a cattle guard in the ground where a gate would be so you can just drive over it. The spaces between the bars are too wide for an animal like a cow or a horse to walk across without getting caught."

"Don't they have cattle grates in Washington?" At first Sam's question sounded like a poking taunt at her lack of country knowledge, but when Alyson turned in the saddle to answer him, she saw a genuinely questioning expression.

"Not in the suburbs," she informed him with a smile.

"I see. I guess there's not much call for them up there." He grinned at her.

"Come on, guys. Let's go before it gets hot." Cat didn't sound like that was the real reason she wanted them to move, but they pressed on anyway.

Within fifteen minutes they had reached a glittering pond. It was much larger than Alyson had pictured and much more pristine—she'd seen in her mind's eye a swamp from the way Cat had made it sound.

Sam, Cat, and Mark dismounted, pulled their reins over their heads, and dropped them to the ground. The horses didn't move. At the most they nibbled at the tops of the grasses. Poco even scraped all the seeds off of the blade of grass with his teeth before pulling the blade off and eating it.

Alyson dismounted and held Chiquita. "Uh, guys?" she asked tentatively.

"Oh, yeah. She doesn't ground tie, does she?" Sam asked from Poco's side.

Alyson shook her head, feeling like even more of an idiot than she had earlier. He undid the rope from his saddle's horn and handed it to her. "Here. Tie her to that tree over there."

After she settled Chiquita safely under the tree, making sure she couldn't get caught or tangled and that the trunk was sturdy enough to be tied to, Alyson joined the others sitting by the pond's dusty shore.

It made her nervous to sit down next to Sam after the previous night. You couldn't like someone you met in less than twenty-four hours, could you? She didn't think so. But for some reason, she was much more self conscious when she was around him. *No*, her mind told her firmly. *No. I do* not *like Sam in that way.*

"Have you decided whether you're going to rope in the rodeo?" Mark questioned Cat.

The girl shook her head, glancing at something unseen in the distance. "Not yet. I probably won't, though. You know, just do penning."

"But you've worked all year for this, you can't just not compete," Sam protested.

Alyson just listened politely. She was still trying to figure out what Cat meant by 'penning'.

"Yeah, but it's not like I won't be competing. I still have penning. And I get to cheer you guys on." A strangely sour look had crept across Cat's face. "It's just no use with Tom and Josh there. One of them always wins. And one of them always makes fun of Buck."

"That doesn't mean you shouldn't compete," Mark put in.

"Yeah." Sam grinned, tossing a sideways smile at Alyson. "You should beat them."

Cat smiled back weakly. "You're right. But then again, you're usually always right about things like this, so it doesn't really matter."

"If you don't mind my asking..." But she couldn't finish. Sam cut her off.

"Oh, sorry. I should've realized you have no idea what we're talking about. It's just that you fit in so well here that I didn't...well, it doesn't seem as though you're new." The explanation took a few moments to make sense in her mind.

Cat rolled her eyes dramatically at his antics and cut in, "Okay, since Lover Boy here can't handle this, I'll explain. In the middle of the summer is the biggest rodeo west of the Pecos. We all compete in high school rodeo. And the name, I'm hoping, is pretty self explanatory." She glanced at Alyson, who nodded. "We do stuff like calf roping, penning, which is were you have to take three specific calves out of the herd and make them go into a pen, and sometimes barrel racing. That gathers most everyone who's anyone around here. Unfortunately, that includes Tom and Josh. They're twin boys from a ranch nearby where they breed roping horses."

"They're not boys. They're both sixteen, I think," Mark corrected.

"And they're probably two of the hottest guys in the state, or so they think." Cat didn't try to hide the disgust in her voice.

"But the two most *annoying* in the state, hands down. They can have any horse they want, any time, and always win with push button horses and fancy new tack." Sam practically spat this sentence as he pulled up a long strand of the golden grass and tossed it to the ground harshly.

"That's an understatement." Cat snorted.

"Are they really rich or something?" Alyson prompted.

"No, but they are really spoiled. They get the first pick of every new horse that their family gets," Mark answered.

There was a drop in the conversation. For a moment, they let the silence cover their thoughts.

"So, this rodeo," Alyson started, her thoughts still on the beginning of the conversation, "Can anyone compete?"

"Sure," Sam jumped in to offer an answer. "Why, you thinking about competing?" This came out as almost a laugh. He sounded as though he were taunting her for asking, but never wiped the encouraging smile off of his face.

Alyson shrugged, undecided. The thought had crossed her mind for a moment. What did she have to lose? She wasn't yet comfortable in a western saddle—after all, she'd only been riding in one for a half hour or so—but she had all summer to get used to it. Most of all, though, the numbing thought that there would be no more dressage training was beginning to take effect. Chiquita was fit and ready for anything. It would be sad to let her talents go to waste.

"I guess I could try. It's two months from now, right? That means I have a little while to learn a discipline. Maybe I could give it a shot."

Cat's eyes widened. "Yeah, that would be so awesome! We could do roping or penning or…" her voice trailed off as her thoughts continued with excitement. Alyson could see it from the changing expressions on her face.

"Barrel racing," Sam finished.

Barrel racing was the ideal sport for Chiquita. She was small and agile, and would be able to spin quickly around the three barrels.

Mark nodded enthusiastically in agreement.

"Yeah!" Cat clapped happily. "Ooh, this is going to be *fun*! We can all teach you, and…and,"

She was about to launch into another series of praises for the plan, but Alyson asked, "Wait a sec—I may not know all that much about western sports but I thought barrel racing was a girl's sport." She looked quizzically at the two guys and then at Cat, who had used the word 'all'.

This brought a chuckle from both of the guys, but Sam was the one who spoke. "Well, it is, sort of. It was first invented to keep wives happy while their husbands were doing other rodeo events. But there are more successful men in the barrel-racing world than most people think."

Feeling slightly nervous about the prospect of learning something new, Alyson mentally reminded herself again that something was only a risk is there was something to lose. And she had nothing to lose.

"Barrel racing it is, then," she said, trying to sound enthusiastic to convince herself that this was what she wanted to do.

Chapter 3

The chords of Garth Brooks' latest song filled the air as they tacked up the next morning. Chiquita was tied to the end of Gabby's pen and Buck was still in his stall while Cat cleaned it. Buffy and Poco were wandering loose through the arena. They stopped every once in a while to sniff at each other, Buffy squealing when Poco got too close and flicking her hind leg at him.

"Just pull it through until it's tight," Sam instructed as she did up the cinch on the old western saddle.

She had been surprised by its weight and knew she couldn't lift it onto the mare herself, so she had asked Sam to do it. He insisted that she mess with the buckles, though.

"But it's not getting tight," Alyson protested, hauling on the strap and wishing the mare wasn't so fat.

"It's because she's blowing out." He laughed gently at her distress but she didn't take it personally. Sam had already struck her as a joking kind of guy. "Just leave it 'till later. We'll finish the rest of it first."

"How come tacking up is so hard?" she asked in exasperation.

Before Sam could answer, the song hit an especially high twang. She could suddenly hear another voice singing along. Mark, who had been cleaning Buffy's paddock, was using the top of the pitchfork as a microphone while wailing along with the words of the song, completely unaware he was being watched. Alyson and Sam both laughed as he pretended to be Garth Brooks.

She prompted, "I have to ask. What's up with the music?"

"You mean, why country?" He raised an eyebrow.

"Well…" Alyson tried to find a way to say this that wouldn't offend him, but she couldn't so she agreed, "Yeah."

He grinned. "Don't worry. You'll get used to it. I guess we listen to it because it's good. Plus it's kind of the official music here. You know, sort of like 'When in Rome, do as the Romans.'"

"I guess I get it. And, for the record, I wasn't saying that because I don't like it. I was just wondering." The recovery seemed useless, but it was true. She didn't hate country music; she just never listened to it.

"Believe me, it's an acquired taste," Cat told her from Buck's stall across from Gabby's. Buck had his head buried in the wheelbarrow searching for tidbits of the hay that the girl had been raking up. His stunted tail swished uselessly at invisible flies. "I didn't like it for a long time," she continued, "and I still listen to other music on my own. British pop is at the top of my list."

This surprised Alyson. She had always figured Cat for a deep down, all-American, country girl. She smiled and turned back to Chiquita. The cinch looked looser. The mare must have let out her breath while she and Sam had been sidetracked.

Sam showed her again how to re-do the cinch and exactly how loose the back cinch needed to be. The breast collar was equally confusing. As with English tack, each piece had a special order in which it had to be put on and taken off, but western tack seemed to have many more buckles and straps. Alyson felt like the only thing familiar was the bridle—and even *that* was different.

The bridle was a curb, meaning the bit had long shanks coming off of the bar that was in Chiquita's mouth that the reins were attached to. The snaffle, which she normally rode in, just had two rings and a bar, the reins then being attached to the rings.

Even the reins were different. They were split, which meant they didn't connect at a point around the mare's neck like English reins. If she wasn't careful, she could drop one and it would fall all the way to the ground, unlike with her dressage bridle. If she dropped the reins with that bridle, they would fall to the horse's neck and no further.

When she mounted up, she again felt as though she wasn't riding her own horse. There was little contact with the mare because of the saddle's large tree and thick saddle pad underneath. And the fenders, which held the stirrups on, prevented her legs from really touching Chiquita's sides. It was as if she were propped up on top of a tower of pillows that swayed and wobbled with every movement.

Sam opened the arena gate for her. Alyson prodded Chiquita into the deeper sand. The mare stopped as they entered and looked around the whole of the large area, but found nothing disturbing.

Alyson didn't know exactly what she was supposed to do. So they were standing in the middle of the arena, what next? So they continued at a quiet walk, but stayed in the center of the arena. Within seconds, Sam rolled a large blue, plastic barrel over to her. Chiquita pricked her ears at it but she stayed placid while Alyson gave her a reassuring scratch on the neck.

"Are we going to run around that or something?" she asked.

"No, I'm going to sit on this. You have to learn the basics first," he explained as a flicker of a smile crossed his face. He lifted himself onto the barrel.

"Thank goodness." Her relief made Sam grin.

"So keep up a circle around me at a walk. Normally, in western pleasure classes, the horse's poll can't be any higher than its withers," he explained as he followed her with his eyes. "But we're not doing western pleasure, so a simple low headset will do."

Chiquita was used to a snaffle, a much gentler bit than the curb she was wearing, and was accustomed to keeping her body rounded for dressage. Alyson had a hard time letting the mare's head stretch down to the correct position. It was much harder than it looked, especially since Chiquita had been doing dressage for the past three years. The bay mare, confused, gave signals that she wasn't sure what Alyson was asking for, but pressed on. Within a few minutes, they were on their way to understanding the concept.

She walked Chiquita around in many circles, telling herself to relax every few moments. Alyson let her reins drop loose, but then pulled them back into her grip again for fear that she was doing something wrong. Where they too loose or not slack enough? Did she look like a fool? Every once in a while, Chiquita would drop her head to the correct position, but Alyson tensed and she began to move in less fluid movements.

After twenty minutes or more of circling both ways around Sam as he made lengthy explanations, he asked them to trot. Alyson gave the mare a little squeeze in the sides and she moved instantly into the quicker pace. But instinctively, Chiquita rounded out her back and bowed her neck, even with little pressure on the reins.

"Pull her back down to a walk," Sam instructed. She thought he sounded pretty frustrated with her but she wasn't certain. "This round headset isn't bad, don't get me wrong, but it's not what I want. I want her the way she is on a relaxed trail ride. You're both a little tense and you use your reins too much. Everything comes from the seat, just as it should in dressage. Let's try again walking."

Alyson felt stupid once again. They were just *walking* and she couldn't get it right. To barrel race she would need to do a heck of a lot more than walk. She couldn't find any way to communicate well with her mare and that frustrated her. Doubt was beginning to creep back into her thoughts. She couldn't do this, so why bother? At the end of the tiny lesson she was practically in tears.

"That was really good!" Sam assured her. He placed his hands gently on Chiquita's reins as Alyson slid out of the saddle. This time Alyson knew she heard forced enthusiasm in his compliment.

"No, it wasn't," she protested, pulling the reins over the mare's neck. "I didn't get that at all. We were going so slow, too."

They led the bay mare out of the arena together. "No, you did really well. Speed makes no difference. It's the same concept you'll use at the gallop." He stopped talking when she walked Chiquita away. After a second of hesitation, he followed her. "At the risk of sounding cheesy, I'm just going to say that 'A journey of a thousand miles begins with a single step'."

"Yeah, well my journey ends right here. I don't want to do this anymore."

Alyson stopped Chiquita by the end of Gabby's stall, all the while fighting back the tears she knew would betray her feelings. She couldn't let herself cry in front of Sam. He'd think she was more of a baby than he probably already thought she was. She dropped her eyes to the ground and set to work on un-tacking Chiquita. But then she realized that even *that* she couldn't do.

"So you're just going to quit after one time?" He sounded astonished. She met his eyes squarely but remained silent as he continued, "The Alyson I know wouldn't do that."

Still holding his stare, she responded coolly, "You don't know me that well."

With that she turned her attention back to all the straps she was going to have to undo. A tear of frustration made its way valiantly down her cheek, but she quickly brushed it away. She was *not* a baby. She was *not* going cry.

Sam took her strongly by the shoulder and spun her to face him. She avoided his gaze as he spoke but didn't turn back around again. "We didn't learn this in one hour. You'd have laughed if you had been watching me rope—well, try to rope—my first calf. Especially since it was made of wood. It took me the whole summer to get somewhere close to the calf. I stunk."

"You're either making that up or exaggerating. Look at you. You're a great rider and your horse is as well trained as a Seeing Eye dog. You're perfect at everything you try," she accused harshly. If she had been her normal self, she probably would have dealt herself a hearty slap.

This time, Cat, who had been listening as she prepared Buck for a ride, jumped into the conversation, "He's not making that up, believe me. He's actually being nice to himself by saying it only took him three months. It was more like a year."

Sam blushed deeply and this made Alyson soften up. She *had* been acting like a baby and she didn't blame him for being forceful with her. No matter how long it took her to master a dressage movement, she always stuck with it—this was no different. She hoped they would forgive her for acting so childish.

Looking down, she said, "I'm sorry. You're right. I was acting weird because this is so different." She lifted her head. "It's just that I never expected to have to leave Washington. I've lived there all my life."

"Not to worry." Cat clapped her on the back so hard she nearly coughed. "Now you've got three good friends to help you through. What more could you ask for?"

She returned the smiles and responded sheepishly, "How about a little help un-tacking?"

"As long as you two come over to my house for dinner tonight. I'm barbequing," Sam said with a haughty tone.

"But what about Mark?" Alyson questioned.

"He's got to work at his dad's factory tonight," Cat explained.

"Well, then, it's a deal." She and Sam shook on it while Cat rolled her eyes to the sky.

* * *

By the time she'd taken a shower and freshened up, Alyson realized it was almost time to go. She rushed upstairs to put the finishing touches on her wardrobe: a pair of beige flared pants and a blue shirt with a sketch of an Arabian horse on it. This was not her best outfit, but she'd learned that in two minutes something clean could become dirty in the country. There was just so much dust everywhere. Standing in front of her mirror in her bathroom, Alyson re-did her sloppy ponytail so that her hair didn't look quite so frazzled, letting two small strands fall and accent her face. She clasped a silver horse necklace around her neck.

"If I don't like him," she muttered to herself as she concentrated on her reflection, "then why on earth am I so obsessive about how I look?"

Alyson herself couldn't answer that question. However much she tried to convince herself of the fact that you couldn't fall in love with someone you met less than a week before, she was still very self-conscious in front of Sam. He was so *nice.* He had been friendly to her since the day they'd first met. Considering the fact that he was a year older than she, Alyson found this amazing. He had a nice smile—no, a marvelous smile. *Okay, so just because you lose your senses every time you see him doesn't mean he feels the same way about you,* her mind told her frankly. *He's a grade ahead of you.*

Alyson was so confused that she decided to push all thoughts of her relationship with Sam out of her mind. She practically skipped through the hallway and into the living room, where her mom sat on the couch reading. Moving into the room, she announced, "I'm going to Sam's now. I'll be back in a little."

"Oh, honey. Can you go get the mail first?" her mother asked in a way that she knew she couldn't refuse.

"Okay, I'll be back in a couple of minutes."

Alyson didn't even wait for a response, but rushed out to the road. It was close to six but the sun was still high and warm. Even getting the mail was a new experience for her. In Washington, the mail was delivered at ten o'clock sharp every morning to the mailbox right outside the door. Here the delivery schedule was much more erratic, and their mailbox was set at the end of a long dirt path close to the barn along with those of the other five houses on the ranch.

It was a short walk, but by the time Alyson had plucked the envelopes and catalogues from the box, she was warm and her heart was pumping. The walk back to the house was also on a fairly steep grade, but she read the mail on the way up to take her mind off the hill.

"To our friends on Rural Route 13," she read off of the back of a catalogue, chuckling. They couldn't be serious. Rural Route 13? That was just about the funniest thing she'd ever heard. Of course they had an address, but they lived in an unincorporated area, which meant they didn't live anywhere with a name.

"Look at me," she muttered as she headed up her driveway. "Who'd have thought I'd ever end up living in a place like this?"

A wave of longing for Washington surged through her. It was hard to believe that it had only been a few days since she'd been there. It felt like years.

She pushed away the awful homesick feeling as she dropped off the mail and left for Sam's, the second to last house on the road. It took her ten minutes to walk to his house, her heart racing the entire time. Alyson willed it to stop galloping and finally convinced herself that it was only beating so hard because she was walking uphill. Not to mention the fact that it was hot.

She made her way up Sam's driveway and rang the doorbell. Cat answered the door clad in flip-flops, a pair of jean shorts, and a short-sleeved t-shirt with the words 'Cowgirl Up' across the front. She grinned when she saw Alyson. "Come on in. You can help with dinner, if you like."

She smiled back and let herself into the house, which was laid out much like her own. The smell of barbecued chicken wafted though the air as Cat led Alyson along the hallway and into the kitchen. Sam's mother was stirring something steaming on the stove while his father set the table. Cat had been slicing tomatoes for a salad, because a work-station on the counter was left unmanned.

"You must be Alyson. I'm Jen." The lady wiped her hands on a spare dishtowel, leaving the pot, and held one out for her to shake.

With a smile and a nod she greeted both parents.

Cat returned to slicing tomatoes at the counter. "Sam's outside if you want to help him. I'm sure he'd appreciate it." She winked pointedly and motioned to the sliding glass door that was cracked open halfway.

Alyson nodded and made her way out the door and onto the cement patio. She grinned as she saw Sam poking at some helpless piece of chicken wearing a messy apron that said 'Kiss the Cook' boldly across the front.

"Hey." He looked up and smiled a goofy smile that would have made a mime burst out laughing.

"Hey." Alyson grinned back and stared at the words on his apron.

Seeing she was watching him so intently, he looked down at his chest and the corners of his mouth creased upwards. "Come on," he pleaded, "Just a little peck on the cheek?"

The air caught in her throat and for a second she couldn't speak. Alyson was so astonished that he'd even *suggested* she kiss him that she thought it was a joke. Why on earth would he want her to kiss him?

At her silence, Sam started again, "Hey, if Cat can do it, you can. It won't hurt. I promise."

She felt a heaviness in her chest. *What else would it be for? He does* not *like me like that. For all I know he and Cat are boyfriend and girlfriend,* her mind scolded her as though she were stupid for not realizing what was right in front of her eyes the whole time. It was obvious that Cat was so close to Sam, so comfortable in his house, that the two of them could be boyfriend and girlfriend. She scolded herself again for thinking that there was a chance of a close relationship with Sam.

A flush filling her cheeks, Alyson rose up slightly onto the balls of her feet and kissed him lightly on the cheek. Her heart pounded in her ears as she let her heels touch the cement again. She could feel the heat rising from inside of her as she did and she hoped he didn't notice how nervous she was.

"Why thank you," he said and then quickly added, "You know, it's good luck to kiss the cook—makes your food twice as good." He skewered a piece of chicken and flipped it over on its other side. It sizzled and spit as it fell.

"Does it?" she asked with a smirk.

"Of course," he explained. "That means the cook makes only the best pieces just for you." The flicker in his eyes sent shivers down her spine.

Was he really flirting this obviously or was this just his way of being friendly? She couldn't tell, but either way, she liked it.

Chapter 4

"Don't be so tense, just let him have his head," called Sam from atop Chiquita.

That day they had decided to switch horses so that Alyson could see what it felt like to ride a well-trained western horse. She'd been riding western for a week and a half, and although she knew she'd improved, she still felt as though she didn't have any control over where the horse was going or how fast it went there.

They had continued to do flat work in the large arena, and for the past three days Alyson had ridden Poco. The gelding was definitely an improvement over Chiquita, so they agreed that she should ride him while Sam worked with Chiquita.

Poco loped along the side of the arena easily, but Alyson couldn't help but think his head was too low.

"He's not going to run away with you," Sam said, and kicked the bay mare forward into a trot to catch up with Poco.

Alyson certainly felt like he was. She was used to keeping a contacting hold on the horse's mouth. She was sure that if Chiquita were allowed to have her head loose and the reins slack she would take advantage of her freedom.

"Okay, it's not as easy as it looks," she responded curtly as she tried to keep her position correct. She sat straight as a slab and only looked forward, shoving her heels down in the stirrups to hold the position.

"That's the thing; you're looking at this as some new thing that's really hard. It's not. Just *ride*."

Alyson understood this clearly, but she couldn't figure out how to let herself just ride. Poco was an excellent horse, there was no doubt about it. It was she who was over thinking everything. *Just ride.*

They made their way around the turn and she relaxed. Just as Sam had taught her, she loosened her grip on the leather that she had been using as a lifeline and softened her seat, making contact with Poco. She lifted her heels slightly, for they didn't need to be that far down, and posted fluidly. The gelding immediately dropped his head to the correct position and lengthened his stride, giving a heaving sigh.

At the change of speed, Alyson grew frightened and regained her reins quickly, hauling on the bay's mouth. Although he didn't want to, Poco reluctantly slowed to a walk. "Sorry," she hastily apologized to Sam as he pulled up alongside her. "I just kind of freaked."

"That's okay, just try not to pull on the reins so hard. You're riding in a curb, which means that you've got something called leverage. For the amount of pressure you pull with, the bit acts in a way that enhances that, pulling on his mouth with more pressure." He put on an encouraging smile for her. "As I said before. Just relax. Poco is *not* going to do anything. He lengthened his pace because that's the trot he's comfortable with. He was telling you that you were riding correctly."

"I just don't get this. I know what it's *supposed* to look and feel like but I can't feel it," she whined, her breath coming in quick rasps from the exercise.

Nervously, Alyson reached down to pat Poco on the neck. *What am I so worked up about? Is it just because I'm riding a different horse? It's not as though I'm like this all the time—and I'm definitely* not *scared. Or am I?*

"Hop off a sec," he instructed. Chiquita stood perfectly still for him, even though his reins were slack, as he talked. How did he do it—how did he make every horse behave for him?

Alyson slid out of Poco's saddle, hitting her feet hard on the sand, and turned to Sam, asking, "What should I do with him?"

"Just drop the reins and leave him." Sam shrugged. Alyson was still blown away by the way all of their horses were so well trained. She never imagined Chiquita being able to do half of what they did. "Come up here."

It took Alyson a moment to realize that he wanted to ride doubles on Chiquita. She didn't quite understand what he was trying to teach her, but left Poco to his own devices and clumsily mounted behind Sam. She could feel the stares of Mark and Cat boring through her back. They must have thought little of her. It had now been almost two weeks since she'd started having lessons and she *still* didn't understand the concept of western riding. If they were going to take this long teaching her simple flat work, how long would it take to teach her to barrel race?

"All right, she's worked okay for me for the past few days so I want you to feel what it's like. If she doesn't improve, we can always put a tie-down on her. That will connect to the cinch and to her nose to help keep her head low. It might help, but it's my last resort, until we actually start barrel racing, I mean. Then you'll actually need it. But right now I don't think you should use devices to make her learn. She needs to understand on her own first."

This seemed to go in one ear and out the other, for half of it Alyson didn't remember. Part of her was so frustrated with riding in general, the rest flustered because she was riding behind Sam. She was so close to him—too close for comfort. She nodded.

Sam kicked the mare into a more enthusiastic walk. By keeping his reins loose and lightly tapping each side of her mouth, he was able to get Chiquita to lower her head to an almost correct position. He encouraged her to sit deep and to feel the bouncing of the mare's head as they rounded the corner of the arena, but it was hard. Her position in the saddle was not conducive to feeling the mare's strides.

Sam showed her how to neck rein, which was basically the same as turning the way she normally did it, although the outside rein encouraged the mare to turn along with the inside one. He explained how riders coined the phrase that Quarter Horses could turn on a dime, and he spun Chiquita in a tight circle to demonstrate his point.

Alyson glanced back at Poco, who was rubbing his sweaty ear up against the arena gate as though trying to scratch off the bridle. Out of the corner of her eye she could see Mark and Cat, smiling as they sat on the top bar of the fence.

Before Sam even had a chance to start a new sentence about reining routines in rodeos, Chiquita caught them off guard. The pepper trees on other side of the arena fence shook with the force of the breeze and slanted to the side. The leaves snapped and crackled like flames. Chiquita was upset by the noise.

The mare snorted and froze for a split second, then pivoted on her haunches, preparing to launch in the other direction. Alyson felt suspended in the air as she flew out of the saddle; that was, *before* slammed to the ground. The world seemed to spin, but she could clearly see Sam wrenching backwards on the reins to keep Chiquita from trampling her.

Please don't let anything be broken, Alyson thought. She had seen many people break bones, or worse, from falling just the way she had. But her whole body hurt like the fires of hell and her breath came in short rasps. *I should never have agreed to do this.*

Her vision came into focus and she found herself staring straight up at the cloudless aqua sky. Pain jumped from bone to bone so she stayed where she was in case her back was broken. At least her common sense hadn't been shaken out of her.

Alyson's heart felt as though it were beating right out of her chest by the time Sam rode back over to her. He hopped off quickly and left Chiquita without another thought, hurrying over to her side. She could hear Cat and Mark rushing to her, as well.

"Are you okay?" Sam asked with a worried look on his face. She had never seen him look so serious, and for some reason she found this funny.

Laughing despite the pain, she retorted, "Do I look okay?"

He sighed with relief and informed the group, "She's got her sense of humor, at least."

"Any broken bones?" Cat leaned over her. She could see Mark soothing Chiquita in the background.

"I don't know. I don't think so. Help me up." Alyson held her hand up and Cat grasped it firmly, helping to pull her to her feet.

Mild pain flowed through her, but nothing more than she normally had when she fell really hard. It took a second for her to straighten up to her full height; she had to balance herself on Chiquita's reins to keep from toppling over again.

"Do you think you can ride?" Sam prompted.

"For a few minutes. I'm going to be a little sore tonight."

The bay was breathing hard, but other than that, didn't seem too stressed. She usually got over things like that fairly quickly. Alyson was more surprised by the fact that she'd spooked at all. But she had to remember that this was still a new place for Chiquita, and horses could get nervous when they were in unfamiliar surroundings.

"All right. We'll just do a little bit more. She needs to go by there again." Sam stated what Alyson already knew—she would have to walk Chiquita by the trees again so that they could make sure the mare knew there was nothing to be afraid of.

Mark gave her an awkward leg up into the saddle while Sam caught Poco and mounted, grinning at her. "Come on. Let's do this before you *really* get sore."

* * *

"Sam, that was stupid. She could have really been hurt," Cat scolded, all the while thinking she sounded too much like her own mother.

"What was stupid?" Innocently, he tossed a potato chip into his mouth, set the bowl down onto the coffee table in Cat's living room, and plopped himself down onto the couch. He switched on the television and reached for the chips again.

Seeing that he was not going to pay attention to her, Cat swooped down and grabbed the bowl before Sam could reach it. "You know what I mean." A stern gaze followed the sentence. She really liked Sam—after all, she had practically grown up with him and his family—but sometimes he could *really* get on her nerves.

"Riding doubles, you mean?" He gave her a guiltless and questioning look. "She didn't understand so I thought I'd show her."

"Yes, but she was doing fine. And you know riding like that is dangerous. Neither of you had any control—and look what happened."

The words were harsh, she knew, but love could be quite a blinding force. Sam had wanted to be close to Alyson, she knew this, too, and so he'd had the crazy idea he needed to help her ride. It had been a pathetic idea, not to mention a dangerous one. If Carole had caught them, they would have been in trouble. She didn't like older riders riding doubles because it put two large people in an uncontrollable situation. As if to prove her point, Alyson had fallen off.

Sam turned his attention to the television. "I guess you're right. But…"

She cut him off by sitting down on the couch and sharing the chips. "I know you're head over heels, but please try to be safe. At the very least."

"You sound like your mom, you know that?" he joked lightly, breaking the depth of the moment.

Cat pulled a handful of chips from the bowl and pretended to throw them at him before eating them.

* * *

Alyson had fallen off horses more than a few times, but this time she had made it count. Even after a hot bath that evening, her muscles ached. Getting into her pajamas was like trying to fit through a barbed wire fence. Even climbing into bed hurt.

The next day she was too sore to ride, so she watched Cat and Mark do some pole bending and barrel racing. Sam, after practicing his slide stops for roping, sat with her on the fence, explaining different points as their friends worked.

They observed as Mark warmed up Buffy. The buckskin mare was very stocky and had wide set legs, which produced a very choppy looking lope. Mark sat the gait easily, rocking with the movements of the horse as he twirled his rope. He sent Buffy through the lope a few times around the arena in both directions before he began to practice his slide stops.

He guided the mare to the short side of the arena and then sent her flying down the long side at a quick gallop.

Sam narrated, "Okay, so picture this. The calf has just been let out of the chute with a substantial head start and they're chasing after it."

Mark did two snappy swings of the rope but did not let it go. A split second later, Buffy slid into a halt and took a step or two backwards. While she was in the sliding position, Mark swung himself from the saddle.

"So he's just roped it. Buffy does a slide stop and stops the calf while Mark jumps off in preparation to tie its legs. Get it?"

"Sort of." She watched as Mark gave Buffy a pat and remounted, preparing to practice the stop once again.

Sam continued to explain for another few minutes, "He'll only practice the slide stops a few times a week. It's hard on the horses' legs. You can easily ruin a horse by slide stopping it too much. But if you use protective boots, are careful, and think about the welfare of the horse, you can have a horse like her last for years."

She nodded at the reasoning and was about to ask a question. But they were both quickly distracted by someone from behind.

"There room for me in there?" A voice called.

They both turned from the perch on the fence to see the owner of the voice. Alyson didn't recognize her—she was a lithe young woman, maybe about twenty-five, with straw blond hair and light brown eyes. She was mounted on a striking chestnut Arabian with a white stripe down his face. Alyson instantly recalled that the horse was Gabby, but she didn't know who was riding him.

"Sure, Lisa," Sam called back to her with his usual grin.

"Are you sure you want an Arab in there with those guys?" she joked.

Sam seemed to suddenly remember something before he said, "Don't worry. You're not alone anymore. I don't know why, but you're not the only one who wants to have an Arab. It's crazy…but anyway. That's not my point. This is Alyson. She has the little bay Arab in the barn. We're teaching her to barrel race."

"Hi, Alyson." The woman smiled and brought Gabby closer to them. "I'm Lisa. And this is Gabby, as you probably know. I'm glad someone else around here has an Arab. They're great horses if you can get one that's not over bred. This one's Polish. I rope off of him."

As Gabby and Lisa practiced, Mark cooled off Buffy and Cat finished her workout. They met by the fence and told her about rodeo for the next hour.

"Watch," Mark instructed, shifting his seat in the saddle. "I'm sure Sam's already explained this to you, but after the rider remounts, the calf has to stay down for six seconds on a slack rope or the run is scored as a no time."

"No, I don't think we got to this part," she responded.

"Well, it's terrible. You've made sure you haven't broken the barrier, roped the calf as fast as you could, and then you just have to sit there for the longest six seconds of your life. It's really bad if you've only tied one loop and a half hitch. You're sitting there hoping beyond hope that the calf won't break the tie and you think the moment will never be over. But it always ends, for better or worse."

They all shifted their gaze towards Gabby as he said this, Sam and Cat nodding ever so slightly. The description was so vivid it sent chills down Alyson's spine.

* * *

The next morning, Lisa and Sam brought Poco and Gabby out to the Sheriff's Posse grounds, a sports complex where riders could pay by the round to calf rope, team rope, steer wrestle, pen, cut, and do almost every other western sport imaginable.

Sam was going to do a training session with Gabby and then practice on Poco. Despite the horse being a flighty breed, Sam liked the way he moved and was willing to take him out to the Posse grounds. He thought the gelding had potential.

Mark tagged along with Sam and Lisa while Cat stayed at Indian River with Alyson to exercise.

"All right, let's start out by trotting the barrels," Cat instructed.

Alyson perked up excitedly. This would be the first time they actually did an exercise involving the giant blue barrels. Before, all they'd done was walk, trot, and lope in circles and other figures.

Cat led off on Buck at a lively trot. The old gelding lifted his tail, but it only flowed a little over a foot from his rump. Still he held his head proudly as they made a wide circle around the first barrel.

Chiquita and Alyson followed at an equally fast clip, careful to make the same wide circle that Cat had. They continued this pattern around the other two barrels and then looped back around to do it the other way.

"This way you'll learn the pattern as it works both ways. You can go to the right or left barrel first, it doesn't matter, so long as you go all the way around the barrel and go in the right pattern," Cat explained as they trotted around the barrels one more time.

After four times, they stopped, not wanting the horses to get bored. Cat demonstrated another pattern that would help with the flying lead change needed between the first and second barrels.

She kicked Buck into a lope in a circle going left. They made a full loop and then began a figure eight path. But just at the center, she slowed Buck abruptly to a walk.

Before the horse could walk forward, she forced the gelding to leg yield, or sidestep, to his left using very little pressure on the reins but more with her seat and legs. This positioned him with his head facing the right and his body bent that way.

With a sharp signal, Cat asked Buck to pick up the lope. Of course, since he was facing the right, he kicked off on the left lead. It all looked very simple.

She repeated this twice in both directions and then began again. But this time, Cat didn't stop Buck in the middle of the figure eight, but just bent him back to the right. In a lackluster but effective movement, the gelding switched leading legs and continued at lope going right.

"Do you see what I was doing? It's a great exercise. If it doesn't teach your horse a great lead change, it'll at least make her more in tune to your aids."

Alyson nodded and heeled Chiquita into a trot. They picked up a lope going right, since Chiquita was easier to work with on her left lead and would most likely change to it easily.

As soon as they reached the center of the figure eight, Alyson did exactly what Cat had done. She stopped Chiquita and leg yielded her three steps to the left, getting the mare to bend that direction. They picked up the lope again, this time on the left lead. It felt just as smooth and easy as it had looked when Cat did it.

"Great! Now try it a few more times."

She did as Cat said and repeated the exercise. Each time Chiquita did it just as perfectly as she had the first time. When they were finished, Cat made her trot the barrel pattern on her own and then they took a ten-minute break. Alyson was as sore as she'd ever been.

"All right," Cat started as they walked the horses along the arena fence. "I know you're tired and sore, but you'll have to deal with it. Pain is a big part of competing regularly in rodeo." She grinned at Alyson's discomfort. "Anyway, since you did so well with that last exercise for the lead change, how about you try it without stopping—you know, going all the way through with a flying change."

Sore as she was, Alyson was excited to try the flying change without stopping. "Okay."

She pushed Chiquita, who was sweaty and breathing hard from the work, into the lope circle one last time. As they reached the middle of the figure eight, Alyson bent the mare to the other direction and gave her a nudge.

Chiquita flicked her ears back, confused, and broke into a trot before eventually picking up the lope once again. She quickly pulled the mare to a halt, feeling frustrated with herself. She must not have signaled correctly.

"That's okay," Cat assured her. "It takes a while for them to get it sometimes. Just trot the barrels again and quit on a good note. The poor mare looks as though she's about to die."

"But what about that exercise?" Alyson asked.

"Something for you to work on," Cat called to her.

Chapter 5

After a few days, a trail ride sounded like the greatest idea she'd ever heard. Although that morning she still needed help saddling up, Alyson managed all the buckles and straps by herself. Chiquita was glad to be going out; although she had enjoyed a few days rest with only one practice shoved in between, she liked being out and working much more than standing in her stall.

Before they rode, they turned up the beat up old radio as high as it would go and pitched in to clean Buck's stall and that of the horse across from him, Gabby.

Gabby, she learned from the previous day's conversation with Lisa, was short for El Gabilan, the name of the mountain range by where the chestnut Arab gelding had been born. She'd also learned that Lisa had a crazy work schedule and often needed Mark, Cat, and Sam to help keep Gabby's stall clean.

The voice of the local disk jockey blared through the air: "Next Friday, Buena Vista Hall, we're having a massive dance party. All ages are welcome, so come out and have a blast. Doors open at seven o'clock and the party goes 'till midnight. Admission is two dollars per person and that includes alcohol-free beverages and other refreshments, plus a night full of country music."

"That was so much fun last time. We should bring Alyson to this one," Mark suggested. He forked a pile of manure into the wheelbarrow.

"Yeah, that's a good idea." Cat said and she turned to Alyson. "All the people from school come to these and they're really fun. We *should* go."

"When is it, again? Next Friday?" Sam asked

Gabby nosed his way into the cluster of people and poked around in the wheelbarrow. Alyson had to push the gelding back before she could continue and hear the conversation.

Cat nodded enthusiastically and turned immediately to Alyson. "We can dress you up like a cowgirl and everything."

Sam rolled his eyes and warned, forking the last pile of manure into the wheelbarrow, "Let's go before she gets any really crazy ideas."

They dumped the manure and left the wheelbarrow by the manure pile so it could be used again. Cat glanced at her watch; Sam went to catch Poco in the pasture and Mark had left to saddle up Buffy. She turned to Alyson and asked, "Do you want to help me turn out Skeeter?"

"Who's Skeeter?" she prompted as they headed for the barn.

"You don't know who Skeeter is? That's right...we haven't had to do anything with him lately. I keep forgetting you haven't been here long."

They reached a middle stall in the barn, across the aisle from Chiquita's, and Cat called out for the horse. As her friend slid open the door and prepared the halter, Alyson watched the fattest horse she'd ever seen in her life head in their direction. He was chestnut with a stripe and a few socks, and his belly swayed as he walked.

As he neared, Alyson noticed that he was missing something—a left eye! In its place was a gaping pit.

Seeing her shock, Cat just laughed. "This is Skeeter, the One-Eyed-Wonder of Indian River Ranch."

They led the horse out of his stall and down the barn aisle, past Tricky Woo, who yapped at them. Alyson asked, "But what happened to his eye?"

"A pitchfork injured it so badly that it had to be taken out. But that was a long time ago. He's twenty-three now. I think it happened when he was only a year or two old."

"Does it hurt him?"

"Nah, it's fine. It just takes a while to get used to seeing him like that, that's all."

They made sure Skeeter was secure in his paddock and made their way back to the main courtyard to get their horses ready. Within a few minutes, they had all tacked up and were gathered by the stable exit.

They headed up a trail through a capsule of trees. A grove of gigantic eucalyptus trees towered around a path wide enough for them to easily ride two or three abreast. The wind rattled through the leaves and branches, creating an eerie feeling of complete natural dominance.

This only lasted a short while, though. The trail bent left onto a road that had probably been used years before any of them had been born. Only for a short time could they ride four abreast, for the trail turned again and rapidly disintegrated.

Cat, still at the head of the train, stopped Buck and turned her seat in the saddle so that she could speak. "We're going up into the woods. The trail stays pretty thin, so Alyson, we're going one by one. We don't think you're a baby or anything, but we're going to make sure you stay in between us."

Alyson nodded. She knew that the least experienced riders were usually placed in the middle, but she didn't take offense at this. After all, she had never ridden on this trail and did not know what to expect.

Cat righted herself and heeled Buck forward up the slightly sloping trail. Mark followed suit, closely trailed by Alyson and then Sam.

The trail shakily followed the line of a barbed wire fence for the next quarter mile. It dipped up and down and twisted through a group of trees.

They crossed another makeshift road that cut in front of a seemingly deep forest of oak trees. To their right was the vast expanse of cow land, marked only by the occasional fence. Straight ahead lay the forest canyon. To their left the road jerked to avoid going up the steep side of an eroded hill.

"Be on the lookout for animals," Mark warned before they entered. "Besides the occasional stray calf, there are mountain lions, snakes, coyotes and bobcats. They usually don't wander around while we're riding, but it has happened."

This grave proclamation scared Alyson. The closest she'd ever come to a real wild animal was at the zoo, where metal bars separated the animals from the people.

Noticing her distress, Sam jumped in to reassure her. "Don't worry, though. I've never even seen a mountain lion for real—just a bobcat. Pardon the pun, but they're real frady cats."

Alyson grinned at the stupidity of the joke, more or less comforted, and they continued. The path was windy but fairly easy for the horses to navigate. The trees opened up to reveal a hidden world, a kingdom of vegetation, while still guarding the golden grass of California's fields.

Despite this, Alyson found herself feeling the ache of her bones more than the beauty of the area. Her tailbone was pounding from sitting in the hard western saddle. This translated quickly into pain in her back and neck. She endured this for a while as they made their way up three twisting paths before she called for them to stop.

"I'm too sore to ride. I need to walk for a little before my butt turns to scrambled eggs."

"We can turn back if you're in pain," Cat offered. Alyson was grateful, but she didn't want to mess up the ride for everyone.

"No." She shook her head vigorously. "No, I'll walk. I'll be fine. I need the exercise anyway."

Sam looked doubtfully at her but didn't utter a word. Alyson slipped from the saddle and unclipped her helmet (Carole implored them to wear helmets while out on the trails). She hooked it onto the saddle's horn and pulled the reins over Chiquita's head. They pressed on this way for another half an hour, chatting in a lively manner.

As they rounded a turn, out of the bushes jumped two frightened deer. They bounded in front of Buck, who just balked and watched them go off into the distance.

Chiquita didn't respond as well. She'd never seen a deer in all the years Alyson had owned her, and probably not even before that. The bay mare twirled, practically jerking the reins out of Alyson's hands, and tried to bolt into the grass on the side of the trail.

Not wanting to let the mare go loose on the trail, Alyson dug her feet into the ground to try and counteract the force of the mare. She was dragged about ten feet off the trail before something caught her and she couldn't help but let the reins slip through her fingers.

Chiquita flipped her head, happy to be free of the pull, tossing the reins in all directions. She ran only a few more steps before her hoof caught one of the split reins and sent her tumbling to the ground. Scattering dust everywhere, she scurried to her feet and set to pacing up and down the side of the area, the hill being too steep to climb.

Alyson fell to the earth with a *thump* while Sam heeled Poco into the tall grass to catch Chiquita. Pain blasted through her and for a moment she didn't think she could get up. Whatever had tripped her was still gripping her leg, and it felt sharp, even through her jeans. She could taste the blood in her mouth and her head was spinning from the heat. For a moment, she couldn't see what was going on, just a flash of many different colors. Taking a deep breath, she sat where she was for a second. Her head felt as though it were buzzing from the inside.

After a moment, she regained her vision to see Sam and Poco near her. Chiquita's reins were attached to the gelding's saddle horn. Sam hopped off the bay and came to inspect her leg. She could hear him curse silently, feeling his anger well up from around him. Alyson felt his grip on her leg, but not much more. A steady throb had begun to develop in the area and she could barely feel anything else.

"Don't move," he told her, breathing loudly. Sweat had begun to bead on his forehead and a drop had slipped down his cheek.

She wanted to make a joke about not being able to move anyway, but all she managed to do was shake her head.

"You're going to be fine, there's just a barbed wire fence wrapped around your ankle. It's pretty rusty, so I'm going to try and break it about a foot from here and untangle your leg. It looks like you have a pretty nasty cut, but nothing more than that. I just don't want you getting any of that rust in your body. So just sit still."

He sounded as though he knew what he was talking about. Alyson wouldn't have objected if she could.

Mark and Cat left their horses ground tied and approached to help with the horses. Mark took Poco and Cat untied Chiquita from the gelding's saddle, taking them both back over to the trail. Chiquita needed to be walked out and soothed—she was still as jumpy as a cat in a doghouse—and checked for injury.

Sam snapped the old wire easily. It practically crumbled in his hand as he gently unwrapped it from her leg. "Nothing to worry about. It's not deep at all, just a scratch."

Alyson had come to her senses, although she was exhausted from the heat and could easily become disoriented again. "Thanks, Sam."

"No sweat. I carry a first aid kit in my saddlebags for situations just like this. I'll go get it and be right back." He spoke to her as though she had just been in a car accident and she didn't know where she was or what he was saying.

Alyson sat, taking deep breaths as Sam left. With a little bit of trouble, she managed to twist her body around to drag a pretty heavy rock closer to her to that she could lean back on it. As she rolled it towards her, flattening the tall grass, her headache returned. Once again she felt that buzzing feeling from inside of her, a rattling in her head.

But no, it wasn't her head that was rattling. Alyson sat up like a shot and spun her head around to see that she had unearthed a snake. Where the rock had been sat a fairly short but thick snake with a distinctive rattler adorning its tail. Her legs froze and she couldn't get up to run. She willed them to move—she *had* to get up. The world spun in slow motion.

Just as she felt a sharp pain jab through her bare arm, her knees unlocked and she was able to pull herself up and rush over to Sam, limping slightly on the leg on which she had tripped.

"She's been bit!" Alyson could hear Cat exclaim, grabbing her and supporting her weakened knees. Sam turned like a startled Thoroughbred and rushed over to help lift her.

"Rattlesnake?" Mark inquired, jumping to help. For a second, she saw two of him moving towards her, but her vision cleared within the next moment.

Sam nodded and once again cursed under his breath. He took her arm forcefully and turned it so he could see the bite. Two fang marks dented into her skin, blood bubbling up from one. "It got her. More likely than not, she's been shot with venom. We have to get her to the hospital. Now!"

Alyson blanched and almost fainted, tears streaming down her face. How far were they from the barn? They had to be at least two miles away. Maybe even further.

"Come on," Sam guided her to Poco's side. He did not want to put her on Chiquita. The mare was still excited and he couldn't take the chance that she'd spook again. It would be hard enough for her to ride Poco back to the barn.

She could barely feel his hands on her sides trying to help her into the saddle. Her mouth and lips tingled, like the tingling that came about from hitting your funny bone on something. And once she was steady in the gelding's saddle, she felt as though she were going to throw up. But when she looked at the ground to do so, she nearly toppled head first out of the saddle.

Cat started as she saw this and hurried to place a steady hand on Alyson. "You have to stay on. It's the easiest way to get you home. Stay awake and you'll be fine. Don't fall asleep."

Alyson's head spun violently and she couldn't tell what was ground and what was air.

Sam continued in the most serious voice she'd ever heard and would ever hear him use. He mounted Chiquita, clutching Poco's reins, and instructed, "Hold onto the horn and *don't fall asleep*. You'll get really nauseous, but hold on tight. We're going to the barn and then I'll drive you to the hospital."

Cat's steady and comforting voice continued soothing her as the gelding began to walk. Alyson rocked along to Poco's steady gait, Cat's hand rested on her thigh as she walked along the trail. Mark rode Buffy and led Buck. The horses seemed to sense that there was something wrong, for Buffy made no attempts to kick at Buck and the gelding made none to nip at the mare's flanks.

"The trail's too dangerous to go much faster than this, but we'll have you there soon."

The rest she didn't hear. Her arm throbbed, and she could, out of the corner of her eye, see that it had begun to swell. It took all her strength to grip the saddle; all her power went in to staying atop the horse. The world rocked and pitched with every step. And she was suddenly very cold, chilled to the bone.

* * *

Alyson vaguely remembered the rest of the ride back to the stable. She remembered the steady drone of Cat's voice, Mark helping her into Sam's pickup, and Sam shaking her to stay awake, but not much more.

She remembered a doctor's voice and her parents rushing into the hospital room. And she remembered lying, exhausted, on the couch in the living room, paying no attention to the blaring television.

Alyson worried about Chiquita, although she knew her friends would take good care of her. What occupied her mind the most, though, was Sam. He'd been so great to take her to the hospital, to care for her when the fence was caught around her leg, and to make sure she stayed awake. How did you thank someone for saving your life?

* * *

The next morning dawned hot, but Alyson was glad to experience it. Her arm was bandaged, and aside from a little soreness, it didn't hurt much. She was tired from the medications and the emotional stress, but her parents allowed her to go to the barn as long as she didn't ride or work.

Her feet sounded too loud on the pavement as she walked down to the stable. The heat rose from the cracked cement, but settled at a comforting temperature around her. A lizard raced across her path; the day was a day like any other, but it felt completely different.

Alyson's mind raced, trying to rehearse the words she would say to Sam, already knowing she would fumble. Over the days she'd tried not to like him as more than a friend, but it was hard. He was so sweet, and handsome, and... he was right behind her!

"Alyson?" Sam's voice stopped her in her tracks.

Oh, great, she thought. *Now what do I do?* Fate had a funny way of working things out. She had only worded less than half of the thanks she felt.

"Oh, hi." The words sounded dumb as they left her mouth.

She waited for him to catch up with her and they walked in pace with each other. He started, "I went to your house to see how you are, but your parents told me that you'd just left. I figured I'd join you."

His smile as he said this made her skin melt into her bones.

"You're making this hard for me, you know." The straightforward approach seemed the best at that moment, and she prayed that it wouldn't be too sudden and too stupid.

"What?" He sounded slightly devastated, which dug a hole in the bottom of Alyson's stomach.

So much for the direct approach.

She continued, hoping to untangle her words, "You...Sam...do you realize what you did?"

"Did I do something wrong?" Sam wasn't that dumb. Deep down, she knew he was just playing with her. He was trying to avoid the point because he wanted to be modest—it was obvious from the expression his eyes held.

"No, of course not. It's just...you were so great the other day that I don't...I don't know how I'll ever thank you."

He shrugged, putting forth a small smile. "Let's see...I would settle for 'I am eternally grateful for the heroic rescue...'" His smile lapsed into an impish grin.

Alyson smacked him in the arm. "I'm serious," she countered, fighting a weakened argument. "I just can't figure out...what can I do? I have to do *something* to thank you."

"Nothing. You don't need to do anything. Everybody gets a free lunch once in a while."

"I don't know. I don't think that saying thanks is sufficient. I mean, you guys have been so great to teach me how to barrel race. Then you have to go and save my life." She waved her arms for effect without knowing it. "I can't just sit here and take all of this."

"See, that's your problem. There are nice people out in the world that don't always want something back. You do stuff for us everyday...like cleaning Gabby's stall and helping us with our horses and being our friend. Convinced?" He made her look at him.

"No, not really. But I understand what you're saying, I guess." Alyson looked away.

"So, when are we back in training? The rodeo's getting closer by the second," he asked light-heartedly.

"I dunno. My parents said I couldn't ride for a few days—after that I'll be riding again. But no more long trail rides," she warned.

"How long is long?" Sam played with her words.

“Nothing where I can get bitten by a snake again.”

“Well, I hate to break it to you, but there are probably snakes in your own backyard.”

“Oh, thanks. I really needed to know that. You’re not very tactful, you know that?” he teased.

“Oh, I do.” By the time he’d finished his sentence, they were at the entrance driveway to the barn.

CHAPTER 6

Over the next week, they worked on building up Chiquita's muscles for barrel racing. Cat set up a line of poles for them to practice weaving through. Buck went first to demonstrate the objectives of the lesson and to give Alyson an idea of what she needed to work on.

Sam, who had done the many times on Poco, zipped through the poles. They rounded the last one as though they were turning on a dime. Poco was incredibly supple.

Mark demonstrated how to start learning to do poles by trotting in a long zigzag pattern. He encouraged Alyson to go through them and instructed her to take them at a walk first to get a feel for how far apart they were.

Tentatively, she moved Chiquita through the poles. They seemed pretty far apart, but she knew that if she were going faster, they would all blur together. Chiquita also had a hard time turning right around the last pole; she bulged her shoulder out and tried to make a ten-meter circle around it.

"Don't worry about that. It's just because she hasn't done anything like this before. We'll get her nice and flexible," Mark assured her. He galloped Buffy through the poles to demonstrate again, whipping around them so near to the poles that it looked as though he would knock them over, but he never did.

Mark smiled his encouragement as Alyson trotted Chiquita through the poles once more. They completed them better than they had the last set.

After this, Alyson worked on the flying lead change exercise. It took nearly a week of repeating the exercise before she got one real flying change, even though she nearly fell off in the process.

This was how practices went. If they didn't work on poles or around a few barrels, they would do flatwork for at least two hours. This usually included going around the large arena five or six times each way per pace. When she didn't ride, she would work Chiquita in the round pen on the long line.

The practices tired her, but they were fun. And she couldn't help but notice the muscles Chiquita was developing in places she never had while doing dressage.

On the Thursday before the dance, Cat suggested they all take a trail ride to cool out after a workout. Alyson was tentative, but Cat finally convinced her to accompany them to the frog pond.

They left the barn four abreast, Sam softly humming the lyrics of "Ocean Front Property" by George Strait. Poco's ears flopped as he listened to his partner sing.

Cat chuckled as she watched them. "I don't think Poco likes your voice," she told Sam, trying to control her laughter.

"Yeah, neither does Buff." Mark laughed and glanced at Alyson.

"Okay, okay. It's a good song, I guess I shouldn't maul it completely." Sam gave Poco a hearty rub on the neck as they crossed the road with the cattle guard on it.

They rode at a walk up the slight hill and stopped by the banks of the small pond.

"How did you teach them to ground tie?" Alyson asked as she dismounted and slipped the reins over Chiquita's head.

Sam answered the question. "It's not that hard. So long as horses understand what you want, it's pretty easy to get them to learn anything. We can help you teach Chiquita, if you want."

She smiled and nodded. It would be so cool to be able to leave her horse loose. She undid her throatlatch, slipped the reins through so they wouldn't dangle to the ground, and redid the latch. Pulling the extra halter over the mare's head, she brought her over to the oak tree and tethered her to the firm trunk.

They all found seats on the dusty ground by the shimmering water.

"The dance is going to be really cool," Cat started. "The only downside is that Tom and Josh will probably be there."

In all the events over the past few weeks, Alyson had completely forgotten about the twins from the other ranch. They couldn't be that bad, could they? Her friends seemed to be really upset about them, but she thought she would give them a chance.

"They're such flirts!" Mark exclaimed.

Sam nodded vigorously. "Yeah, they see a girl and they automatically think she was made for them." He turned to Alyson and warned, "Don't be suckered in by them. They might act like they like you, but they don't."

"But they must like *someone*," Alyson protested. She was having a hard time picturing them in her mind's eye. She didn't know many twins and the only ones she knew were girls.

"They'll find someone they really like eventually, but now they're just in it for the physical aspects of the relationship, if you know what I mean," Cat replied. She rolled her eyes and sighed.

"Do they do everything together?" Alyson prompted.

"Almost," Sam answered. "But it doesn't matter. Don't mess with them. They're bad news."

Mark and Cat nodded in agreement. For some reason, she couldn't imagine that two people could be all that bad, but she accepted it and changed the subject. "So…what else do I have to learn before we start to really barrel race?"

"Balance," Cat put in quickly. "You have to have balance and speed at the same time. It's not all that complicated, but it's something you have to think about."

"And speed…you have to be fast. You can get a running start but you have to cut the turns quickly. They say a horse that turns is better than a horse that can run." Mark said, demonstrating the barrel racing process by drawing it in the dust.

"You have to actually make it all the way around the barrel. You can touch it, but if you knock it down you get five seconds added to your time. That hurts. Oh, and then there's that lead change between the first and second barrels."

The dialogue overwhelmed her, but she thought that she understood most of it. Dressage required accuracy and precision; barrel racing required speed and balance. She could master it. No, she *would* master it. "I think I get it. What are you all doing for the rodeo?"

Cat looked down, bearing the weakest look she'd ever seen Cat wear. The girl shook her head. "I don't know yet."

The words echoed in Alyson's mind for a moment. All of a sudden, she remembered the conversation that they had on the banks of the pond before. "But you can't just not compete because of those two guys," she protested.

"Yeah, and you can't leave us without a penning team this year," Sam told her, giving her a grin of encouragement. "We have to win, beat the pants off of them. Besides, we've always done penning."

He turned to Alyson, quickly explaining how they would be assigned three cows to cut from the herd and run into a small pen, hence the name of the sport.

"And with all of us competing, they won't have a chance in any event." Mark put a cheering hand on her shoulder.

"Well, I would still do penning, of course, like I said before. But I don't know about the roping. Why enter? Those guys always rope perfectly. They're practically unbeatable." She was still looking down, disheartened.

"Okay, how about this," Alyson suggested, taking a deep breath. "You rope in the rodeo and I'll learn how to rope. I'll even rope in a competition one day. That is, provided I don't kill myself learning."

Cat lifted her eyes, which held a hint of a smile, at this. "You would really do that?"

"Yeah." She tried to look as though learning to rope wouldn't faze her, because it really did. But she wanted to help her friend more than anything, and she knew Cat would like to watch her learn something else.

Cat grinned. "It's a deal."

* * *

Cat ran her fingers through Alyson's hair, glancing to the mirror as she pulled it back. She held it there for a moment, then let it drop, humming under her breath the words to Toby Keith's song "How Do Ya Like Me Now." "How about a French braid?"

Alyson turned from her stance in Cat's bathroom and prompted, "Can you do that?"

She shrugged. "I can try."

"Okay." Alyson faced the mirror again and watched as Cat picked up the brush. She studied her outfit—a light purple short-sleeved shirt with a v-neck, dark blue jeans and cowboy work boots that hurt her feet. The bandage on her arm had gotten gradually smaller until a few days before, when it had disappeared. But she still had an ugly scar where the bite had been that she wished wasn't so noticeable.

She wanted to look absolutely perfect that night, which was why she was letting Cat do her hair. She was too nervous to do it herself.

The older girl ran the brush through her hair a few times and set to work. Alyson stayed quiet for a moment, listening to the music coming from the radio in on the counter and then asked, "So what exactly is this that we're going to?"

"A dance—you know, exactly like school dances but totally country music," Cat explained

"You mean, like, line dancing and stuff?" This came out with a slight hint of fear. Alyson didn't know how to line dance, and she did not want to embarrass herself in the process of learning.

The words brought a muffled laugh from her friend. "*I* don't even know how to line dance," Cat informed her, pulling the braid tighter at the top of her head as she worked. "Some people do, but we probably won't. This is just going to be good music and a good time." She finished the phrases to the song and began to mouth the words to the new song that had started playing.

"Good." Alyson didn't try to conceal the relief in her voice.

Cat twisted the braid one more time and tied it with a hair band. "There, how do you like it?" She stood, proud of her work, smiling.

"Excellent." Alyson grinned.

Her hair was pulled back evenly into a neat braid and two wispy strands accented her temples. Cat had secured the braid with a fancy western clip.

Soon, they were ready to go. She checked her watch; it was nearly five thirty. Sam and Mark were taking them out to dinner before the dance and had said they would meet at Cat's house around that time. However, the guys and Lisa had taken Poco, Buffy, and Buck to the Posse grounds so they had to park the trailers, put away the horses, and get ready at Sam's house.

Sam's white pick up glided along the barbed wire fence-line and into Cat's driveway just as the two girls left the house to wait for them. The sun was still high and it was warm as Mark and Sam hopped from the truck.

"Good evening, ladies." Mark produced a very proper British accent that made them both laugh.

Sam pulled his hands from behind his back and handed a blood red rose to Alyson, stating properly, "I would be honored if you would be my date tonight."

Alyson knew that she blushed to the exact shade of the rose she now held, but she managed to answer in a calm tone. "It would be an honor for me, as well."

All the while her heart raced. This was just a joke, but it was awfully realistic. If she glanced up at Sam's eyes she could see the spark that she'd seen a few other times. Maybe this *was* real. Or maybe she was way off base.

"Ahem?" Cat clearing her throat interrupted her thoughts. "Romeo over there at least got a flower for his date, are you going to do the same?"

She was glaring pointedly at Mark. Alyson was amazed at how serious she could be when she was joking, which made it all the more funny.

Mark shuffled over to the fence that bordered Cat's driveway, picked a half dead poppy, and he handed it to her. She sighed, accepting the flower. "I guess it'll have to do."

They all squeezed into Sam's truck. Mark and Cat filed almost too quickly into the back so that Alyson could sit in the front.

They stopped at the local burger joint and filed back out of the truck. Alyson had eaten there once with her mother, and found the food good.

"I have an idea," Cat started while they waited for their food.

"For what?" Mark asked.

"For Alyson's training...well, more for the rodeo. Chiquita's going to have to get used to flags, loud music, the roaring crowd, you know."

"You're right," Sam pointed out. "I keep forgetting she's not used to the same stuff our horses are so familiar with."

"What are the flags for?" Alyson asked. She took a sip of her drink.

"Usually at rodeos there are drill teams, like trick riders and flag bearers, who ride with all sorts of flags," Mark explained. "It takes a lot of talent to ride with them, since they're so heavy, so we won't be doing that for a while. But the horses have to be used to them because they're all over the rodeo grounds."

"Yeah, and loud music is definitely a factor—along with the voice of the announcer booming trough the speakers," Cat added. She glanced up to see if their food was ready so she could bring it to the table.

"There's also another thing we like to do in the crowd and that's to stomp feet on the bleachers. It's kind of a rodeo tradition...sort of like applauding but bigger." Sam's eye caught the sight of their order and jumped up before anyone else could to go get it.

Cat rolled her eyes. "Might as well let him act like Sir Lancelot for a little while."

They grinned as Sam returned with the burgers and fries. They ate and continued chatting about Chiquita's training and what happened at rodeos.

Cat and Sam explained in depth about roping and Mark talked about team penning. They agreed that they would give her a roping demonstration next week.

By the time they'd finished, Alyson was ready to pay for her part of the meal. There was only one problem: Sam wouldn't let her. When she tried to grab at the check, he quickly swiped it away.

They climbed back into the truck and he drove out to the hall where the dance was being held Music blasted from the tiny hall while people filed in and out. They were greeted by the chords of Faith Hill and people of all ages having fun.

"Shoot. Look straight ahead." Cat turned and cringed the moment they walked in the doors.

It was a very old and very small hall with a wooden floor. Alyson could see a refreshment table at the back of the room. With it was a set of chairs, sparsely populated by a few people who didn't look like they cared for dancing or music.

Mark paid for their entrance and asked as they walked in, "What?" But he saw what she had been cringing at even before Cat could utter the answer. "Oh."

Alyson glanced up to see two people she immediately recognized as the infamous Tom and Josh. They hadn't been kidding when they'd told her they were handsome. They were probably the closest thing to Brad Pitt the town would ever see...and there were two of them! They certainly didn't look mean, but she had learned never to judge a book by its cover.

Sam rolled his eyes away from the two and guided her to the other side of the room. "Do you want something to drink?"

She shook her head. They had just eaten and she was stuffed. But she wanted to dance.

"Come on, let's dance. I like this song." With slight trepidation, she grabbed his hand and pulled him out onto the dance floor.

He didn't try and stop her, but let himself be dragged into dancing. By the time they had finished dancing to a slew of fast songs, Alyson was out of breath.

She'd taken turns dancing with Mark and Sam, as did Cat. Although she was incredibly tired, the energy of the place was contagious, and she couldn't stop dancing.

After a few more quick moving songs, the disk jockey decided it was time to play a slow song: Toby Keith's "You Shouldn't Kiss Me Like This". Alyson was prepared to sit this one out; she was tired and she didn't figure anyone wanted to slow dance with her. But before she could, Sam tapped her on the shoulder.

"May I have this dance?" he asked very properly. She felt her cheeks flush at the handsome expression on his face and the heat rising throughout her body.

She thought of declining the moment he asked. But then she figured: why not?

"You may," Alyson answered formally as the music began to play.

Sam spun her towards him and grasped her gently as they swayed to the music. Her mind was racing. At first she thought of the song and the lyrics.

She shuddered at the thought and the fact that Sam was holding her so close. Alyson could even have rested her head on his chest as they danced, but she didn't dare. All too soon, the minutes were over, and the song was over; the moment they'd shared was over.

"Thank you for the dance." Sam bowed formally to her as their bodies parted, Alyson feeling quite warm.

"Thanks." She smiled at him shakily and said, "I'm kind of warm. I'm going to go outside for a minute."

"Do you want something to drink?" he prompted again with a slightly concerned tone. She figured it was because he was worried about her health after the rattlesnake incident, so she agreed.

"Yeah, thanks."

She made her way out the door and to an empty bench she'd spotted outside the hall. Her heart and mind were still racing with thoughts and emotions she didn't think she could feel. Sam had actually *danced* with her—they had been so close together. And yet their relationship was so far apart. She'd only known him for a short while and he surely wouldn't become involved with someone he barely knew.

And why should she care? Alyson had been trying to convince herself since she'd met him that she didn't like him, but why was it so hard to believe? She didn't want to like him. He was a good friend to her and was helping her train her horse, nothing more.

"Oh, I don't know. I'm so confused," she muttered out loud.

Sam's return with a cup of punch interrupted her thoughts. "Here."

"Thanks." Alyson was grateful for the drink, gulping it down as he sat down next to her on the bench.

He sighed and gazed up at the stars.

She held the cup to her lips for a prolonged moment, in hopes of not having to say anything in the uncomfortable moment. Did he want her to say anything? What would she say if she *did* say something?

But Sam spoke first, in a contemplative tone. "What do you think is up there?" His head was tilted towards the sky.

"Huh?" The question struck her as so foreign that she didn't think she'd heard right. Before he could answer, though, she formulated a response to his question. "Oh, I don't know. I guess I'm usually so worried about what's down here that I don't think about what's out in space."

"I mean, are we so self centered that we think we're the only ones in this huge expanse of universe?" The question was so philosophical she practically had to pinch herself to make sure it was really Sam talking to her.

"I guess we are. We're so busy looking for other life forms that we probably don't realize there is someone out there looking for us. They might even think we're not all that intelligent..." Alyson let her words drop as she looked up at the sky.

"That would be so weird—so sci-fi." He chuckled at the thought, which made her grin to herself.

The chords of another slow song, "Tell Her", by Lonestar, began to fill the night air, even outside of the hall. The sounds floated over the strawberry and lettuce fields, soaking into the night.

"Do you want to dance?"

"Here?" he asked, surprised by the sudden idea. They had just danced...and outside? Why didn't they just go inside and dance?

"Here. Under the stars. It'll be special," he said as he stood up.

He gave her an encouraging smile and took her hand, pulling her to her feet.

"Okay." Her voice was soft as she stood up weakly and met his firm grip.

Sam held her tightly to him as they glided slowly across the cement walkway outside of the hall. The hum of the music was gentle and it relaxed her. This time, she rested her head on his chest, feeling more secure than she ever had. Despite the fact that he was a year older, he had never treated her as anything but his equal.

Normally, older students at school tended to tease underclassmen and not take them seriously, but Sam had done none of that. After only a month she knew she could tell him anything and not get a sardonic laugh from him for opening herself up.

Maybe Alyson really was completely lovesick, head over heels, whatever you wanted to call it. Maybe the relationship would never happen. But at that moment she didn't care. Swaying in Sam's arms made her feel as though she were on top of the world. Already this had been one of the most amazing nights of her life.

The song trickled to an end, leaving them still in each other's arms. It was almost as though they hadn't realized the song was over.

"How about we go for a trail ride tomorrow?" Sam's comment was out of the blue, although it didn't seem so.

"Where to?" he asked, pulling away so they stood out of each other's grip, but still close together.

"Have we taken you up Murrietta hill yet?" he asked.

Alyson shook her head.

"Well, there's an amazing view once you reach the top...although you have to get past the fact that the place is named after a criminal."

"What criminal?"

"Well, more than one criminal, really. Joaquin Murrietta and his gang, including others related to him. They stole hundreds of wild horses from around here in the 1800's and drove them down to Mexico and sold them. They used the trails up on top of the hills to drive the horses."

He grinned devilishly at his own knowledge.

"Well then, I guess that sounds good." She smiled at his strange comment about the Murrietta gang and then said, "Come on, let's go inside."

She didn't want to end the moment, but she was worried of what her friends might think about them being alone for so long. And maybe Sam really didn't want to spend all that much time with her outside alone.

Alyson started to turn around, but Sam stopped her with a touch on the arm.

"Wait." He bent down and gave her a quick kiss on the cheek. It was incredibly close to her lips without being forward and without actually touching them. When he pulled away, he said, "*Now* we can go inside."

He escorted her back into the building, Alyson feeling dazed and happy. He had *kissed* her. He had actually *kissed* her! It was not on the lips, albeit, but it was a kiss. She was so jaded that she had to sit down the by the refreshments and have another cup of punch.

Sam grinned at her and went off to dance with Cat for a little while. Alyson plopped herself down on one of the chairs with another cup and drank it all it one sip.

She replayed the events of the evening in her mind. Sam really must have liked her if he was willing to go all out like this on their...well, it wasn't a date, or was it? Yes, it was a date. He wouldn't have kissed her if it weren't. Or was he just trying to make her feel good?

"Excuse me?" A smooth, young male voice rang out in her head and broke her out of her thoughts.

When she looked up, he almost backed off. It took her a second to realize who it was. The light hair and deep blue eyes of Tom (or was it Josh?) looked quite different close up. Rather sheepishly, he started again, "Um, I'm Josh...I know your friends...and I noticed that you weren't dancing...and I wondered if you would mind dancing with me. A pretty girl like you shouldn't be sitting out." The last words sounded very cliché for some reason—or at least they sounded pretty stupid.

But adrenaline was still rushing through her and she figured there was nothing to lose. Josh didn't seem all that evil from their brief encounter, and it wasn't as though she and Sam were going out. All he had done was kiss her on the cheek. They weren't bound to each other.

Alyson grinned and stood up. "I would love to."

She placed her hand on his outstretched palm as he led her onto the dance floor.

They danced to a quick song that didn't require closeness, and then the slower Dixie Chicks song "Without You". Josh was forward but not rude, and allowed her to position herself for the slow dance. He kept up a little small talk while they danced, asking her about her life and what she liked to do. She found him quite agreeable to chat with. She even found that she might like to have him as a friend.

When the song was over, Josh guided her back to the refreshment table and got her a cookie. She took it gladly, hungry from dancing. They talked for a little while longer.

Before they could delve deeper into conversation, Cat practically pounced down her back. Alyson almost choked on her cookie, but regained her composure and glared at Cat.

"Sorry, am I intruding?" Cat asked with mock innocence. Josh gave her a dark look.

Alyson knew that her friend was doing this on purpose. She knew that Cat didn't want her to be talking with Josh, but she was upset that she interrupted the way she had.

"Yeah, actually," Alyson answered sourly.

She tossed an apologetic glance at Josh, who was being nice despite the distraction.

"I'm sorry, but Sam's got to go."

She grabbed a cookie and took a bite, guiding Alyson rather forcefully away from Josh.

She glanced back to Josh, waved a shortcut goodbye, and proceeded to get angry at Cat. "What was that for? He was being perfectly nice to me! You didn't have to drag me away."

"No. You don't understand. Trust me, you don't know Josh, or Tom. He's nice to you now, but he doesn't really want to know you. They want easy girlfriends," Cat warned. "Stay away from him. He's bad news."

Alyson shrugged and let herself be dragged to the pick up. It wasn't as though she was doing anything more than talking and dancing with Josh. She wasn't going to go out with him. Whether or not Cat knew she liked Sam was irrelevant, anyway.

The ride home was quiet, but the thoughts that pounded through Alyson's head were loud. She thought of the kiss, of the warning Cat had given her, and of Sam again. He hadn't said anything to her for the rest of the night, not even when they reached her house. All he did was wave a silent goodbye, a perplexed look on his face.

Chapter 7

Sam didn't show up at the barn the next morning. Alyson had saddled up Chiquita by ten o'clock and was waiting by Buck's stall with Cat while Mark worked Buffy in the arena.

Buffy loped easily along the side of the arena, appearing as though she was reading Mark's mind. He didn't seem to give her any cues, yet she carried out movements with precision accuracy.

Chiquita pulled her head to the ground and shuffled the dirt with her lips in hopes of finding shoots of grass or other edible plants.

"He promised he'd take me up Murrietta hill," she told Cat, leaning on her arms on the bars of Buck's stall while Cat groomed the short-tailed Appaloosa gelding.

Cat just kept her eyes pinned on her work and shrugged. "Maybe he doesn't feel like it. Last night was tiring." The excuse was so empty that she knew she didn't have to press Cat anymore. Alyson wouldn't get an answer, even though she was sure that Cat knew what was going on.

Sighing, Alyson led Chiquita to the arena and mounted. She practiced the poles for a little while, trying to make Chiquita turn faster. She worked on flying lead changes. And then she cantered around a few barrels. She also let the mare lope loosely for about five minutes.

But her mind was not in the practice, and although they did very well, Alyson wasn't fully there to appreciate it.

Although she wasn't completely into the exercise, Alyson did notice how the mare seemed to be doing what she asked much quicker and with ease. Her muscles were well toned and she could gallop for longer than she could when they were just doing dressage. She loved the powerful burst of speed that was pushed forth when the mare took off at the high pace.

For a precious moment she was so caught up in what she was doing that she forgot about Sam. Her momentum was broken when she finally saw his truck coming up the road. It rumbled along as it normally did, but did she detect a hint of sadness? No way—cars could *not* be sad!

Alyson pulled Chiquita to a walk and waved to him as the car passed them. She received no wave in return and sighed. Was Sam just one of those people that kissed and ran, never saying a word to you afterwards? *It wasn't even a real kiss*, she reminded herself. *Just something between friends*. Maybe he felt bad for doing it.

But then again, a friend would wave when another friend waved first. There was definitely something fishy going on with Sam. Even Cat was acting strangely. Was it the fact that she'd danced with Josh? That wasn't such a big deal at all...or had she violated some kind of friendship thing? Mark hadn't even said much to her that morning, come to think of it.

She circled Chiquita around to the gate. Once they'd reached it, she positioned the mare so she could slide the latch open and swing it open. The mare waited obediently for her to give the signal. Then she sidestepped easily to close the gate She wasn't even breathing hard, but she was impatient to go back to her stall.

Alyson rode her at a brisk walk to where Sam had parked his truck outside the gate of the large pasture in the courtyard. She pulled Chiquita to a halt when she met him unlatching the gate.

"Oh, hi," he muttered without being prompted. The words were dry and lifeless.

"What's wrong?" Alyson asked with obvious concern in her voice. Chiquita shifted her position, forcing Alyson to move her back before she could listen for answer.

"Nothing." He tried to make his voice sound light and even. "Nothing's wrong. I'm just going to go for a ride."

"I'll come with you. Remember, you promised…" But she couldn't even finish the sentence.

Sam turned his back to her, cutting her words short. "No. I need to go alone. And don't bother following me." He called out to the gelding, who came in from the field at a lively trot, ready for a treat.

Alyson watched as he haltered Poco, let him nibble a carrot in his pocket, and re-latched the gate. Only when he led the horse over to his trailer without a word did she leave. She could take a hint.

She let Chiquita amble back to where Cat was still grooming Buck. She was pulling every scrap of dirt from his mane and tail before she washed and shampooed them.

"What's up with Sam? He's going on a ride alone." Alyson asked as she reached the stall. She slid from the saddle, giving Chiquita a well-deserved pat.

Cat shrugged, turning to her this time and lying through her quite convincing teeth. "Sometimes he likes to do that. It's no big deal. He just needs to be alone."

As if to emphasize what she had just said, Alyson could hear Poco coming up the driveway behind them. Sam had bridled him, and he was heading out bareback. He hadn't even realized that he was ignoring one of the biggest rules for the young riders: they weren't to go out alone, much less bareback and without a helmet. Even Alyson knew that.

Sam and Poco were almost trotting by the time he headed up the road and turned off on the trail to the frog pond.

"Really. It's not big deal," Cat repeated, although Alyson could hear muffled concern in her voice. "He's just a little upset. Something must have happened at home."

She knew this wasn't true—she knew it was something she'd done. "Not only," Alyson grabbed a helmet and put it on, pulling Chiquita to the fence and mounting again, "is this stupid. It's also dangerous. I'm going after him before he gets himself killed."

"No…Alyson. Don't. It'll only get worse. Don't worry, he can take care of himself." Cat's words were no use—Alyson was already heading out at a trot before she'd finished.

She was forced to slow to a walk before they began their slight climb up the trail that led to the frog pond. After all, she didn't want Chiquita to end up with a broken leg. She settled with a lengthy stride at the walk.

Poco's footprints were fresh, even on the solid ground. The grass was bent away where Sam had veered off the path. It was obvious where he had headed.

Different thoughts bounced across her mind. Subconsciously Alyson subconsciously slowed Chiquita's pace to give her thoughts time to voice themselves inside her head. What had she done wrong? It must have been something she did that was irking Sam so much. Why else would he not speak to her? The night before he had kissed her, and that had meant a lot. Or at least she thought it had. Maybe it didn't mean as much to him as she thought it did.

The events of the evening replayed in her mind. The only thing she could think that might have upset Sam was the fact that she'd been talking to Josh. But what did that matter anyway? It wasn't as if she'd shared her life's secrets with him. All she had been doing was having fun.

The trail dribbled away and the pond appeared in front of her so quickly that Alyson almost started with fright. At first she couldn't spot Sam or Poco in the scenery, but within a moment she could see the gelding ground tied near the oak tree where she normally tied Chiquita. Sam was perched between the spread of the lowest branches, looking out over the open land. He was positioned so that she almost thought his back was turned to her.

Apparently it wasn't.

"Go away! I told you not to follow me." The words sizzled like a leaf under a magnifying glass in the sun.

Alyson was cut by them, but didn't let it show. She dismounted in a fluid motion and approached the tree. "Are you crazy? Is that all you can think about? What if something had happened to you?"

Sam jumped from the tree before she could reach it, giving her an acid glare and startling Chiquita. He walked over to Poco as though he were about to mount again, but didn't.

Alyson secured Chiquita's rope around the tree and drew nearer to Sam. She didn't say anything, but waited for a response.

Every word he said hurt. "Well, it didn't, okay? Just leave me alone. This has nothing to do with you."

"Apparently it does!" he yelled to him, coming around the other side of Poco. He tried to avoid her gaze but she bore her eyes down on him. It was like trying to catch a wild horse with just a halter from the huge expanses of the open land.

"No, it doesn't. Just leave it. Leave me alone. I need to think." Sam picked up Poco's reins, lifting the gelding's head.

"About what? What's wrong?" Alyson pleaded, positioning herself so that he would have to move around her to leave.

"Nothing. Just…" Incomprehensible words seemed to spit from the corners of his mouth before could form the rest of the sentence. "Just leave me alone."

He tried to shove past her but she stopped him. "Please, Sam, just tell me what's wrong. If it's something I did, I want to know. I'm trying to be a good friend!"

If looks could kill, Alyson would have been dead in a moment from the look that he threw her way. "If you're really that clueless then you might as well just go back to Washington and leave us alone."

His words hit her hard. She couldn't think of one thing that she'd screwed up that badly. Maybe she never should have left Washington in the first place. Maybe she really was clueless. Hot salty tears began to stream down her cheeks.

For a moment, Sam seemed to soften up as he saw her cry. But when she glanced up at him, his expression became stony. He pushed around her, flipped the reins over Poco's neck, and mounted in a quick movement. "Don't bother to come after me this time."

Ooh, Alyson thought as Poco's swift strides ate up the ground. *Ooh. What's his problem? How could he speak to me like that?* She was fuming mad, frustrated, and hurt as she made her way around the tree to where Chiquita was tied. She took a deep breath and leaned back against the tree. She had to calm down before she rode back, or she would run the risk of blindly riding into danger.

Alyson let her body slide to the ground beside Chiquita's feet and cried. She let the tears fall for a while before she made an attempt to wipe them away. Chiquita lowered her head as if to comfort her.

She smiled and stroked the mare's white star. Chiquita was better than any guy any day. She listened and didn't talk back. She didn't judge by appearances. She wasn't hard to figure out. She was a loving friend that would never betray her.

Alyson stood up slowly, wiping the dead grass off of her back and seat. She gave the bay mare a quick hug and remounted. They rode back to the ranch at an easy walk, Alyson trying to enjoy the warmth of the day and the beauty of the land.

Upon her arrival by Buck's stall, she knew Cat was trying very hard not to give her an 'I-told-you-so' look. She just turned from tacking up the Appaloosa and asked, "How'd it go?"

"Not as well as I would have planned." She dismounted, trying to stay relaxed, and led Chiquita into the arena. She pulled off her saddle, propped it onto the fence, and then took off the mare's bridle. Chiquita shook her head and dropped down to roll in the deep sand.

Alyson left the arena, latched the gate, and slung the bridle over the metal bar. "What do you know about this whole situation?" She prodded Cat, walking over to the pipe stall and leaning on the bars.

Cat focused her attention intently on the buckles of the saddle as though she didn't know what she was doing, wiping her gaze away from her friend. She shrugged. "Nothing really. Sometimes Sam has these…uh…mood swings." Cat was desperately trying to escape her words as she made up the explanation.

Alyson could see right through her. She wanted answers. And now Cat knew something and wasn't telling. Why did they want to hide this from her?

"Cat, please. I really need to know what's going on. It's something I did, I know it, but I don't know what." The words came out as a soft plead. She could feel the tears springing to her eyes once again.

The other girl turned with a pained expression on her face. "I can't tell you; you have to understand. It's nothing personal, but I promised Sam. I swore I wouldn't tell…"

Alyson set her gaze squarely on Cat's, her eyes brimming with salt water. She figured that the stare would wear the other girl down. It took a few moments, but Cat relented.

"Okay, fine. But don't tell him that I told you. I didn't really want to get caught up in this—but Sam and I are like siblings. I can't help getting caught up in his problems. It started at the dance. Well, it started before that, but it peaked at the dance. Sam has got a major crush on you…and when he saw you dancing with Josh and talking with him, he got mad."

"But I wasn't…" Alyson began to think out loud, but ended the sentence abruptly.

Now she understood what was going on. She had been right once that morning, but hadn't wanted to think it could be possible. She understood why Sam was mad at her but was growing upset that he had left her to figure out the situation. Alyson couldn't quite figure out if she was ecstatic that he had a crush on her or was still mad at him. Confused emotions shot through her. "Thanks, Cat. That was a really big help."

She turned away with a forced smile and headed for the arena to bring in Chiquita and her tack.

"Wait…what are you going to do now?" Cat asked with concern in her voice. It was obvious she regretted spilling the secret.

"I'm going to wait for him," Alyson told her firmly, promising once again not to tell where she'd gotten her information.

She slipped the bridle off of the gate and slung it over the saddle horn. Hefting the saddle off of the bar, she carried it into the barn and headed for the tack room. When she had placed the saddle on its correct stand, Alyson continued back down the aisle to get Chiquita.

A clipped yapping sound scared her until she realized that Tricky Woo was approaching her. Smiling, Alyson bent down to pet the fuzzy little dog, but it could not bring her out of her emotions. She needed a long time to think.

As she walked back to the arena to catch Chiquita and bring her into the barn for a grooming, thoughts bounced around her mind. Yesterday she would have been overjoyed to learn that Sam liked her as more than a friend, so why didn't she feel that now?

And what about Cat? She'd always secretly wondered if she was Sam's girlfriend. But she'd stopped thinking about this possibility because she never saw them acting like she was. Maybe she would be after today. Alyson tried to imagine what life would be like without his contagious smile, his quips, and his caring personality. It wouldn't be the same. And maybe now she had lost her friend to their fight. She could have hit herself.

Alyson haltered the Arabian mare and led her from the arena. The sweaty mare tried to rub her head against Alyson, but was shoved away. They headed through the barn aisle until they reached the mare's stall, where she tied Chiquita to the bars of the stall and set about grooming her.

After about twenty minutes of brushing Chiquita with a currycomb, Alyson continued with a soft brush. She took her time. Just as she was making swipes across the bottom of the bay's barrel, she could hear tentative footsteps behind her. Turning, Alyson recognized Mark. She figured he would wave and walk by, using the barn as a shortcut to get somewhere else.

But he stopped at Chiquita and rested his hand on the mare's side. "Alyson?"

"Oh, hi Mark." The words exited her mouth softly.

"I want to talk to you—Cat told me you were upset." He sat down on her tack box and beckoned for her to sit next to him.

"No," she said as she sat, "I'm not upset…"

Mark gave her an unbelieving look. "Look, I know this whole weekend has gotten off to a really confusing start."

"Tell me about it—Sam acts like he hates me and then I find out its because he likes me. I don't understand!" She looked down, not knowing why she was pouring her heart out to a guy she wasn't very close to.

He chuckled at her comment. "Believe me, he's just about as confused as you are. Practically as soon as he met you, he was smitten. Cat and I set last night up so that he could take you and I would take Cat. We figured maybe both of you would realize that you had feelings for each other." She blushed as he said this, remembering the kiss Sam had given her after they'd danced.

"But it kind of backfired when he saw you dancing with Josh. I wouldn't expect you to understand why he was so upset You haven't been here long enough to get to know Josh or his brother. He and Tom have sabotaged our chances of winning at the rodeo, hurt our horses, not to mention making fun of Cat because Buck isn't the most beautiful horse in the world."

Her breath caught at the explanation. Why on earth would someone want to deliberately hurt another person's horse? Mark continued. "What I'm trying to say…in a roundabout way…is to give him a chance. He really likes you and he'd be hurt if you at least didn't stay friends."

The tears were springing down Alyson's cheeks now, both out of sadness, happiness, and confusion.

"Thanks," she breathed, leaning forward to catch Mark in a hug. He pulled away quickly, explaining that he wasn't a touchy-feely type of person, and she had to laugh. Afterward, he stood up awkwardly, gave Chiquita a pat, and went to go groom Buffy.

Soon, Alyson had finished Chiquita's grooming and given her a bucket of grain. The mare gobbled it up and thanked Alyson with a gooey kiss as the girl stepped into the stall to retrieve the dirty bucket. After rinsing it and putting her brushes away, Sam still hadn't returned.

Sighing, Alyson sauntered across the barn aisle and peeked through the bars and into Skeeter's stall. The one-eyed horse turned his head to her and focused his good eye on her. She scratched his chestnut muzzle and left him, headed for Sam's trailer in case she'd missed him.

She found the area empty, but the trailer's tack room door was unlocked. Alyson pulled open the familiar door and sat on the edge of the tiny space. She pulled her knees to her chest and leaned against the wall. It wasn't the epitome of comfort, but it was a seat; a seat where she was sure she wouldn't miss Sam.

While she waited, Alyson reviewed Mark and Cat's words in her mind. She couldn't believe what her friends had said about Josh. He'd acted like a gentleman the previous night, not like someone who would childishly sabotage someone's chances of winning at the rodeo.

The minutes drew themselves out into an hour and a half. It was only then that Alyson could hear the familiar sound of Poco's hoof beats on the hard packed ground. Suddenly, her heart froze and the blood running through her veins turned to ice. She had no idea what to say, and

Sam was approaching fast. All the blood that had iced over took her by surprise and flooded instantly through her body as she heard Carole calling Sam's name.

Alyson peeked through the hinges of the door to watch what was happening. The stable manager looked upset and was holding the Quarter Horse's reins. In an angered tone, she ordered Sam, "Dismount, now. What did you think you were doing?"

He did as ordered and then weakly answered, "I just took a little ride."

"You went out alone, not to mention bareback and without a helmet. You and your horse could have been hurt. You know better, Sam!" Her hands moved to her hips and she stood in a threatening stance. Alyson felt a pang of sorrow for Sam.

"I'm sorry. I just…wasn't thinking, I guess." The words were flimsy and didn't hold up his argument. But then, it didn't look as though he was trying to counter her words.

"You should be sorry. You'll be here tomorrow afternoon to help me repair some fences." With that, she handed Poco's reins back to Sam, who was looking down disappointedly, and hurried off.

He gave the gelding a pat and led him over to the trailer. For a moment, he didn't notice Alyson, at least not until she stood up. He opened his mouth to utter something, but Alyson stopped him with her words. "Cat told me everything." *So much for keeping my promise*, she thought. But the words had just come out.

"Everything?" He raised a calm eyebrow and reached out for Poco's halter.

Alyson nodded. She handed him the halter.

"So? How did you feel when you found out?" He asked as though this was not the secret he held close to him; he asked more like it had been something on the news.

"Glad, I guess." She shrugged.

"Glad. Just glad?" Sam asked as if to check that she'd said what she said.

This brought out a mild chuckle. "You should be glad I don't hate you for what you said to me." Alyson reached into the trailer's tack room and grabbed a brush to help him groom Poco. She handed one to him over the gelding's back.

"Ouch. Point taken. I was being a jerk."

He took the brush and began to swipe it across Poco's barrel.

"Yeah, you were."

"Well, you don't have to agree with me!" He laughed—this was the Sam she knew. This was the Sam she loved.

He ducked under the bay's neck and met her. He took her hands in front of her and held them softly. "I'm sorry. I'm sorry I was so mean to you. I was just jealous. I really do like you."

"And I like you, too." She could feel a happy shiver penetrating her skin.

"Okay, so I'm going to ask you this question again, but don't answer until after…anyway, how do you feel about…?" but he never finished.

He bent forward to kiss her—on the lips this time. She met his advance willingly. They kissed for a moment and then pulled apart, their eyes locked. She grinned and then let out a laugh (it was too close to a giggle than she would have liked to admit).

"Ecstatic," she said, and fell into his arms and held him before kissing him once more.

From behind her she could suddenly hear wild clapping and whistling. Alyson snapped from her dream and looked up. Sam did the same. Mark and Cat were laughing and cheering—watching them kiss!

"You are *so* dead!" Alyson warned and pulled from Sam's embrace to chase after her friends.

Chapter 8

Alyson leaned forward and helped Chiquita round the barrel in one quick, sweeping movement. She pressed her legs into the mare's sides, urging her to gallop even faster to the next barrel.

In a flash, Chiquita switched leads. Adrenaline pumped through her body as they snapped around the second barrel.

Chiquita flicked her ears forward for a second at the long way between the second and third, and dropped off the pace. She could feel the bay hesitate, as if she wasn't sure what to do.

Alyson quickly squeezed her back into the speedier gallop and guided her around the barrel. They just barely made it around without knocking it over.

She pressed her body forward and urged Chiquita to give even more speed. They raced down the arena and crossed the mock finish line. Alyson turned the mare and slowed to a canter, then quickly moved to a trot and a walk.

Alyson caught her breath as they slowed. They had done the pattern three times already that day, and none of them had been quite up to her abilities. It was less than a month from the rodeo and she had been barrel racing correctly for almost a month. She and Chiquita had clocked some competitively good times—she knew when she was on top of things, and that day she wasn't. That was why Chiquita had hesitated.

"You've done better," Sam told her from atop Poco's bare back. He held a stopwatch in his right hand and let his left drop to Poco's withers. The bay gelding appeared to be taking a nap. "Did you feel her slack off between two and three?"

Both Alyson's and Chiquita's breathing was labored; they headed over to where Sam had parked Poco to look at the watch. "I know. And yes, I felt that. She seemed like she didn't know what to do."

"You've just got to keep asking for more. She's got it, she just has to be told that she can go faster," he explained in his most professional voice.

They met at the fence in front of Cat and Mark. Mark had snapped the lead off of Buffy's halter and was letting her graze loose on the dry tidbits of grass around the area while he and Cat perched on the metal arena fence.

"Are you ready?" Cat asked. "The trailer's hitched."

"Ready for what?" Alyson asked.

"We thought you might like to come out to a ranch and watch us rope and pen some calves. We said we were going to take you to watch a demonstration, but we've never gotten around to it," Mark explained.

Her eyes grew wide with excitement. "Of course. That would be so cool." "

Sure, her friends had practiced their roping quite a bit at the Posse grounds, but she had never actually seen them work with calves.

"Okay, well, come on. Put Chiquita away and then meet us back here at the trailer," Sam told her as he hopped off of Poco's back. The gelding held his head down so that Sam could unlatch the throatlatch of his bridle. He re-fastened it over the reins so that Poco wouldn't get himself tangled in them and walked out of the arena. Poco followed him obediently.

Alyson heeled Chiquita through the gate behind them. She dismounted easily and listened as Sam ordered Poco, "Go get in the trailer."

She watched curiously from Chiquita's side to see if the gelding would actually do it. He was a good twenty feet from the open trailer, and all Sam had done was point and tell the horse to get in.

Poco headed calmly for the trailer, but stopped at the step up and turned his head back to Sam.

"Go on," Sam told him. The gelding seemed to nod and stepped up onto the bedded floor of the trailer. He positioned himself diagonally so that Cat could close that half of the trailer.

Alyson couldn't believe what she had just seen. Her friends' horses were constantly surprising her. Laughing to herself, she guided Chiquita around the area to cool her out, and then to the barn to settle her in her stall with her grain.

By the time she returned, Buck had just been loaded into the trailer. Cat closed the two back doors and latched them firmly, checking twice to make sure that the doors were safely closed.

"What about Buffy?" he asked when she returned.

Sam jumped out of the bed of his truck to answer the question. "Well, since it's only a two horse trailer and we don't want to have to make two trips, you two are going to ride two of a friend's horses."

"Whoa, whoa? Us two? I just rode…and besides, I can't rope a cow," Alyson said. Heck, she'd never even *seen* a cow up close.

He laughed lightly and moved closer to her, taking her hands in his comfortingly. "They aren't *cows*, they're *calves*…and what if I kiss you for good luck?"

She smiled giddily. "Then I think I might be able to manage…" They leaned forward to meet in a kiss, but a call made them pull apart.

"Yo, Romeo and Juliet. Would you hurry?" This was Cat once again. She and Mark had put Buffy back in her paddock and were already in the truck.

They both laughed and headed for the truck.

The ride was about twenty minutes down the road that led to the town in the opposite direction of town. They passed by fields of strawberries, lettuce, and artichokes as well as cattle, sheep and horses until they turned down a long dirt road. The trailer turned and bumped alongside a massive pasture.

Alyson spotted a few horses grazing on the golden California grass as they turned once again, this time down a smaller road. They passed an arena with chutes on one end and a regular fence on the other.

"Okay, there's one thing I should mention." Sam explained as he parked the trailer. "This is Tom and Josh's parents' ranch. We wouldn't come here, but it's one of the only places where we can practice with calves besides the Posse grounds, and we don't want the horses getting too used to roping only at the Posse grounds. Besides, a friend of ours boards here since Indian River is full."

Alyson groaned. She still remembered quite clearly what had happened the last time Tom and Josh became involved.

"It's okay, though. We can basically avoid them," Mark explained. "There are lots of other nice people here. And we'll be needing to come back more often now that it's close to rodeo time."

They all piled out of the truck. Alyson stopped to look around. The place was big, bigger than Indian River Ranch, and laid out much differently. A large pasture almost encircled the place, and there was no large barn, just an old wooden shelter in the pasture and a set of paddocks.

The arena was much larger than either of the two at Indian River. One end had two square areas set into the side and a long chute between the two.

"Their family basically runs this as their own ranch, but there are a few people who board here," Mark continued. "A friend of ours, who taught us everything we know about roping, has a few horses here and invited us to come back out to practice for the rodeo. Sam started and did basic training for all of his horses."

Still feeling unsure, Alyson nodded and set out to help bring Buck and Poco out of the trailer. A memory waved over her as she helped open the back doors. Alyson clearly remembered that day they made that deal: Cat would rope in the rodeo and she would learn to rope.

Sam and Cat saddled their horses quickly their tack having been in Sam's trailer. They mounted up and led the way into the stable.

"Hey, Brad!" Sam called excitedly as he spotted a tall man on a light bay horse in the courtyard.

The man turned his horse towards them and trotted over. He was young, perhaps twenty two or twenty three, and he looked like a country music star—brown hair with a short stubble beard and a large golden belt buckle. "Sam! You guys come out to practice?"

When they met, he nodded. "Yeah, we wanted to show our new friend some roping. Brad, this is Alyson. Alyson, Brad. Oh, and that's Buddy." He pointed to the horse.

"Hi. I'm Sam's…uh…" she didn't know what to say. Surely, she was his girlfriend. But she didn't really want to say that, so she just stopped. "I just moved here about a month and a half ago."

"Well, welcome." Brad had a friendly and welcoming smile that made her feel good. Maybe being at Tom and Josh's place wouldn't be so bad.

"Can we use Brooks and Beau?" He asked, shifting his position in the saddle.

"Of course. You know where they are and where the tack is. We're loading some calves in the chute right now. I'll see you over there." He waved and turned the bay in the direction of the large arena.

They headed the opposite direction of Brad and made their way to an area that had paddocks similar to the one in which Buffy lived.

"This is Brooks." Mark pointed to a light dun Quarter Horse gelding that stood asleep in his paddock. "You'll be riding him."

Alyson entered and haltered the gelding while Mark went around the corner to get his horse.

"He's called Brooks because he's dun," Sam began. "Get it, Brooks and Dunn?"

She laughed at the bad country music joke and patted the horse, shaking her head.

"It's true!"

Just at that moment, Mark returned leading the biggest Quarter Horse Alyson had ever seen. The chestnut gelding was easily 17 hands high. He had two loud white socks on his back legs and a blaze that dribbled over his lips. "This is Beau."

"Come on, I'll show you where the tack is." Cat turned Buck and led them over to a large trailer. She dismounted and left Buck ground tied, then opened the door and showed Alyson where Brooks' tack was.

Within minutes they were mounted and ready to go. But before they could head out to the arena, Tom and Josh rode up on two stunning horses: a young black and white paint and an equally young looking dark bay.

With a smirk on his face, Josh pulled his bay up and sneered. "Pathetic. It's really pathetic. You guys can't show up on your own horses because they're not good enough?"

His head bent down a tad to his horse and his brother's. They were obviously of very high quality, but that didn't mean anything as to their abilities.

Alyson was taken aback. This was not the same courteous person she'd danced with. That probably hadn't been the real Josh, she realized. She wanted to return his snide comment, but couldn't think of anything to say.

"Couldn't show up on anything good yourselves, eh?" This came from Sam. She knew he didn't normally like taking out human aggressions on a horse, so she was surprised by the way he belittled the young geldings.

Josh didn't outwardly seem fazed by this, but Alyson could tell that he and Tom had been.

"Would you like to place a friendly bet, then?" Josh moved his bay forward. "Two of you versus us two, two rounds of roping. The winner gets…um…"

"If we win, you guys have to buy us all sodas, hose our horses, and put them away," Cat challenged. It was a friendly bet; nothing big. That was a fair punishment for the losers.

Until Tom spoke up, that is.

"And if we win, none of you compete in the rodeo." Tom looked very pleased with himself.

Alyson almost spoke up, but Sam tossed her a look that told her to keep quiet. What if they lost? All their work that summer would be for nothing. What if they competed anyway? No, they couldn't do that. She'd heard that Tom and Josh had actually hurt their horses before. They couldn't risk it. They should just call it off before it got any worse.

"It's a bet," Sam said, and he pulled Poco up to Tom's paint to shake his hand. "Let's go."

"All right. We'll be back in twenty minutes. We're going to go for a trail ride to warm up, but we'll be back to watch you lose." Their rudeness hung in the air as they trotted up the road.

"What on earth did you just do?" Alyson kicked Brooks up to Poco's side to ask Sam. "What happens if we don't win?"

"Don't worry." His teeth were pressed against each other and his face was set angrily, so angrily that Alyson could see the scene playing in her head to Mark Chestnutt and Tracy Byrd's "A Good Way to Get on My Bad Side". "We won't lose."

* * *

Brooks was a wonderful horse. He put up with Alyson's pathetic attempts at roping a stationary calf made out of hay bales without taking a wrong step. She nearly fell off when she did her first slide stop in a mock calf rope. Sam taught her how to use the piggin' string to tie three of the calf's feet.

"Pigging string?" he asked, making sure she'd heard right.

"No, *piggin'* string. Only two G's," he explained with a chuckle.

"Does roping hurt the calves?" She asked a moment later.

"I wouldn't know, I'm not a calf. I do know that it's a slight shock for some, and sometimes injuries happen, but we always take them to the vet if they get injured. We in rodeo usually respect rodeo animals, although there are a bad few," Sam explained.

She nodded and they practiced once again.

Twenty minutes passed like five. Poco, Buck, and Beau warmed up while Alyson tried to rope and played around with some reining maneuvers. All too soon, they could hear the hoof beats of Tom and Josh's horses as they returned.

"You ready?" Josh asked while they both entered the arena.

Since Brad was there with two other young men manning the calf chute as well as the stopwatch and was within earshot, there was not as much edge to their voices. And they certainly didn't say anything that could have been considered mean.

Sam nodded. Mark and Cat completely ignored them.

Sam was up first. First wasn't the best position to be in at that point. Once he roped the calf he would have to use the piggin' string to tie up three of the calf's legs. And once the calf was tied he had to get back on his horse and let the rope slack. Then, six seconds would tick away. If the knot held and the calf stayed down, his time would be calculated and it would be official.

First was not a good position because the calves hadn't been roped and tied yet that day and would be fresh and hard to tie. He also had to be careful to give the calf a ten-foot head start (since this was a small arena; in larger arena calves got a longer head start) or he would break the barrier out of the roping chute. A small rope around the calf's neck was connected to the barrier, and after ten feet it would snap and the barrier would open. Alyson knew she would never be able to do it, but thankfully, she didn't have to. She and Mark were just there to hang out. Mark would practice when they went to the Posse grounds again.

They picked a spot by the rail to sit on their horses as Sam walked Poco into the chute. With one hand he held the reins and the rope as he repositioned his cowboy hat on his head. With his teeth he held the piggin' string. Concentrating intently on the calf that was being loaded, he held Poco.

Once the calf was ready, Sam nodded, and the calf's chute popped open. A split second later he sent Poco flying out of the box. With a toss, the rope fell over the calf's neck. Poco slid to a stop and Sam jumped off, running to the calf, the piggin' string ready in his hands. As if the calf weighed nothing, Sam flipped it on its side and grabbed its front leg, letting the loop on the end of the rope tighten around it.

In what seemed like less than a second, he had made two wraps around the calf's two back legs and front leg. The calf was tied. Sam scurried back to Poco, remounted, and let the rope slack.

6-5-4-3-2-1. The calf stayed down. Sam had been quick: 9.7 seconds and he had not broken the barrier. That was pro.

Brad's friend raced over to the calf, let it free, and then returned the piggin' string to Sam, who was pulling his rope back into his hands. "Good job." He nodded to Sam as they split off in opposite directions.

Next it was Cat's turn. She posted in the saddle, flipping her rope around, and made her way to the chute. The piggin' string was clamped down in her mouth.

She watched as Brad prepared the next calf, Buddy standing behind him. As soon as it was ready, she nodded.

Buck and the calf flew out of their chutes, the calf just a few steps ahead. Cat flung the rope expertly at the calf, but the rope didn't catch around its neck. Buck slid to a stop, and Cat jumped off: she had the calf by its front foot. Hurriedly, she ran to flip the calf before it freed itself.

With force, she flipped the calf on its side and sat on its hindquarters, the rope connected to Buck's saddle pulling its front leg forward. Unhappy at Cat's attempt to tie its legs, the calf kicked with its back legs, barely grazing her face. This didn't faze her. She tied the knot and remounted Buck, letting the rope slack. The knot held, but seconds later Brad told her that she'd broken the barrier. She would have ten seconds added to her original time, which was slightly slower than Sam's because of the kicking calf. 20.4 seconds was the end result.

Tom was the next up. As he rode his paint around the arena, he had a smug grin on his face that Alyson couldn't quite decipher. She knew he was happy that they had gotten a bad time on the last calf, but this grin was different. It was obvious that he was already counting on them not competing in the rodeo. But the round was not over and there was still one to go.

She held her breath the whole time Tom rode. The brothers' horses behaved perfectly, but the horse couldn't do it all. Tom still had to rope and tie the calf.

The breaking of the barrier nearly scared Alyson off of Brooks. She hadn't been prepared for the sudden start. She hadn't been prepared for how perfectly Tom roped, either. His run was textbook style and definitely as fast as the pros: 7.5 seconds. That was fast enough to win at televised rodeos that were actually held in places with populations of more than 2,000.

Sam didn't say anything but kept his eyes focused on something outside of the arena. He mindlessly flipped his rope around, deep in thought. Alyson knew he wanted to win this more than anything. After all, Josh was the one that had caused their fight, both brothers had always been consistently mean to them, and there was more at stake than whether they would compete in the rodeo. Their pride was at stake.

Fortunately, Tom's other half didn't perform quite as well. The calf got a good head start on him and was tough to tie down. He came out of it with a time of 13.5 seconds. That was still a much better combined time than Sam and Cat's by about 7 seconds.

Sam was up again, and Alyson could tell he was spitting mad and ready to win. He didn't outwardly show that he was upset, but she could tell. He looked the same way he had the morning he'd been mad at her.

Sam rode into the chute and positioned Poco at the back so he could watch the calf being loaded. It was important for Poco to be focused on the calf, or their run might not go well. The calf was the same one that Cat had roped.

He nodded. Careful not to run against the barrier, he shot out after the calf. In a split second, he had tossed the rope. Poco slid to an abrupt stop and began backing, knowing the calf had been hooked.

Sam was at the calf in half the time he'd taken to rope it and flipped it on its side equally as fast. Maybe the calf was tired, maybe it knew that it wasn't going to get away with anything, but it didn't even try to struggle. With one motion, it was tied. Sam remounted quickly and let the rope slack. The calf didn't try to get up and the knot held for six seconds. His time was blistering fast and he hadn't broken the barrier.

This was when Alyson understood Mark's explanation of the six second slack from that night they were watching Gabby. She wasn't even competing and she was as nervous as she'd been all summer waiting for Sam's time.

Sam retrieved his rope and piggin' string himself so that Brad's friend could write the time down on the tally. 7.2 seconds. Alyson knew that was the best time they would see that day,. From what she'd heard from Sam, she knew that was just about record time. The grin on Sam's face only confirmed what she knew.

He trotted Poco over to her and positioned the gelding so that he could throw his arms around her and kiss her just as passionately as he'd roped. "My good luck charm," he whispered into her ear, and she smiled giddily.

He hugged Cat and high-fived Mark after that, giving Cat a thumbs-up. As she rode Buck to the chute, she called back to him, "How the heck am I supposed to top that?"

Laughing, he answered, "I don't know. Try!"

Cat's run was stunning. Although it wasn't quite as fast, it definitely made up for her previous run. They finished with a combined time of 16 seconds flat for their second round.

They didn't even have to watch Tom or Josh's round. The brothers were so shaken up that Tom missed the calf completely, and Josh fumbled to tie a knot that didn't hold. Two no times on the parts of Tom and Josh left Sam and Cat the winners.

And those sodas were the best that any of the four ever tasted.

Chapter 9

Alyson's phone rang at nine a.m. on Thursday morning the week before the rodeo. They had been back to Tom and Josh's and the Posse grounds four or five times to work with the calves in preparation for the rodeo. She was exhausted every day and sleeping late when the phone rang.

Lazily, she meandered around the kitchen counter and picked it up. "Hello?"

"Hey, is it you?" It was Sam's voice on the other end. By the fuzzy quality of the phone, she could tell he was at the barn.

"Of course it's me. Don't you know what I sound like?" he joked.

"All kidding aside," he began rather shortly, "you'd better get down here. Buffy's dead lame and we don't know what's wrong."

"She hasn't broken anything has she?"

"No, no. She's just limping like it would hurt to even put a pound of weight on her foot. Carole's not here, but we called her."

"All right, I'll be there in a minute."

Alyson rushed through breakfast as though she were inhaling it, got dressed quickly and left a note for her mom. Without a second thought, she ran out of the door and down the road to the barn.

When she arrived, Mark was holding Buffy on a short lead and looked distressed. The mare held her left front leg out in front of her and stood on her right. Her body was flecked with sweat from the pain; she must have been suffering for a while.

"I think it's an abscess coming in," Sam stated to the group. "There's nothing in her foot."

"I still think she could have stepped on something and still be feeling the pain," Cat reasoned.

"Well, whatever it is, there goes our penning team. At least she's not fatally injured." Mark sighed despondently.

"Yeah, if she was, Carole would have been out here as quick as she could drive. Buffy might even have kicked out at the fence and jarred her leg really bad," Sam offered, giving the mare a pat on the neck.

"What happened here?" A voice from behind made them all turn to face the newcomer.

Alyson recognized her quickly. It was Lisa, Gabby's owner. This was one of the handful of times she'd seen her in the last few weeks.

"Buffy's lame," Cat explained. "We don't know what happened."

"Oh, I'm so sorry. That's too bad. I know you guys really wanted to ride in the rodeo together." She offered her sympathy and came closer to look at the buckskin mare.

"Yeah, but I guess there's always next year." Mark still sounded terribly depressed, although Alyson knew he was trying to hide it. He was concerned about his horse, but he was still upset about the rodeo.

There was a moment of silence, and then Lisa began, "Wait a minute, what am I thinking? I have a perfectly good horse right here. Why don't you ride Gabby? I mean, if you could stand to ride an Arab in the rodeo."

Mark brightened obviously but tried not to let it show. Instead he said, "I couldn't. He's your horse."

"I insist. I wasn't planning on riding him this year and you deserve to have a horse to ride. He's been roped off of and has quite a bit of cow sense for an Arab. And I won't take 'no' for an answer," she persisted.

Alyson knew that Mark was too polite to accept on the first try, and she had a feeling that Lisa did, as well.

This time Mark glanced up and grinned. "Thank you so much!"

And so it was settled.

* * *

The group practiced penning with Poco, Buck, and Gabby at the Posse grounds, while Alyson brought Chiquita to get her accustomed to the rodeo environment.

Mark and Gabby worked together like a dream over the week, but Buffy didn't improve. The vet visited and determined that there indeed was an abscess coming in; they would have to wait until it popped before Buffy could be ridden again.

Chiquita's flying lead changes were perfect, Gabby and Mark were on fire, and Poco and Buck were on top of their game. And there was only one week to go.

* * *

Mike Walker's "Honey Do" played through the open window of Sam's pick up and sounded into the air. The morning of the first day of the rodeo had dawned with a warming sun that brought heat through the afternoon. By four thirty, the sun was still warm but not quite as powerful as it had been at noon.

"A little closer…closer…perfect." Alyson guided Sam as he backed the truck up to his two-horse trailer.

She felt excitement surging through her despite the fact that she would not be competing or even bringing Chiquita. The rodeo was made up of four days: two evening competitions on Thursday and Friday, and then two daytime competitions, and the horse parade, on the weekend, the finals being on Sunday.

On Friday she would bring Chiquita to get used to the rodeo grounds, but she would only be competing on Saturday. If she made a good run, she would make it back on Sunday. But this was her first actual rodeo and her friends were competing. She couldn't help but be excited.

He shut off the truck, cutting off the song mid-chorus, and got out to go hitch the trailer to the truck.

"Do you have the tickets?" he asked her while he worked.

"Yeah." She reached into the pocket of her jeans just to make sure they were still there. Sam and Cat's family got box seats every year whether they planned to use them or not. That night, their parents would be in the stands where they could wander if they wanted to. Most likely, though, they would probably watch from the backside of the arena. "They're right here." Feeling like she would burst if she just stood there, she said, "I'm going to go check on Lisa and the rest."

"All right, I'll see you back here in a few minutes."

Alyson practically skipped across the stable, passing Chiquita's stall on the way to where Lisa's trailer was parked. She felt bad that she had to leave the mare at home, but she knew she would need time to herself that night to get used to the rodeo.

She met Mark and Cat sitting over the wheel of the trailer with a binder-full of CD's. "Okay, so we have Mark Chestnutt, Tracy Byrd, Brooks and Dunn, Rascal Flatts, Chris Cagle, the Dixie Chicks, Lonestar, Garth, Reba, SheDaisy, Faith Hill, Toby Keith, Brad Paisley, Martina McBride, Gary Allen, Vince Gill, Charlie Daniels, Shania Twain, Tim McGraw, Alan Jackson, Travis Tritt and Trick Pony." Cat went through the CD's with precision. "I think we'll survive four days of rodeo."

"I think you'll get sick of country music after four days of rodeo." Lisa laughed as she came around the corner. She smiled warmly at Alyson.

"Sick of country music? I don't think so." Mark shook his head. They all laughed. Neither of her friends looked nervous despite the fact that they would be competing in team penning that evening.

"Everything ready over here?" he asked.

Cat nodded. "Gabby's loaded. I'll go get Buck. Does Sam have the trailer ready?"

"Uh-huh," Alyson answered with a nod of her head.

"All right. Here." Cat shoved the CD's into Mark's hands and walked with Alyson in the direction of Buck's stall.

"So, do you like your outfit?" her friend asked with a smile. Cat looked natural wearing jeans, cowboy boots, and a cowboy hat.

Alyson felt like a total fool. Cat had let her borrow a pair of her old work boots, and she had invested some money in a pair of Wranglers. Her shirt was her own, a light blue short-sleeved shirt. And she wore a cowboy hat. Well, not just yet. Maybe after two days of rodeo she would feel better wearing it. "Truthfully I don't think it's quite me...are you sure no one's going to laugh?"

"Believe me, they'd laugh a lot more if you didn't look like this. Going to the rodeo's like going to a different world. So forget about it and just have fun."

"Fun? I'm so nervous I don't think I can stand having fun."

"Nervous? Geez, I'd hate to see what you're going to look like on Saturday when you actually have to compete." Cat laughed at her own thoughts as they reached the trailer.

Poco was wandering around the area trying to find any tidbits of grass he might have missed, while Sam forked some soiled bedding out of his trailer.

When Sam saw them coming, he stopped and looked up. "You ready?"

"Whenever you are," Cat answered easily, reaching into her pocket and taking out a horse treat. She handed the cookie to Poco, who gladly accepted it.

"Okay, let's see really quick. We have the tack," Sam began.

"Check," Cat ticked off.

"The wraps and boots."

"Check."

"First aid kit, glue shoes, hay nets, hay, etcetera."

"Check."

"Grain, hay, and extra buckets."

"Check. We're ready to go. I'll grab Buck."

Alyson watched as Sam told Poco to go into the trailer. The horse ignored him at first, but when he repeated the command in a louder tone, Poco lifted his head and snorted.

"Let's go," Sam reminded the gelding. Poco seemed to sigh and plodded slowly to into the trailer.

Sam tied Poco in the trailer and shut the barrier so that Buck could follow. The three friends piled into the truck. Mark was riding with Lisa and Gabby.

As the engine started, the song "Laredo" by Chris Cagle began playing on the radio. Laughing, Sam called out to them through the open window, "Wagons ho, everyone, it's rodeo time!"

* * *

People bustled everywhere. Alyson had never seen so many people in one place. She didn't even know there *were* that many people in this town. She stared, gaping, out the window as men and women wearing incredibly tight jeans buzzed around in cowboy hats.

As they passed the front of the rodeo grounds, Alyson could see a group of people carrying signs and calling out to everyone who would listen. They were laminated and boasted disgusting pictures of half-dead cows and horses. "Rodeo is violent!" their signs screamed.

Alyson was sobered by the signs. She'd never thought about this before. And her friends had never mentioned anything about cruelty in the rodeo. But then again, they were rodeo people.

"Is what they say really true?" Alyson asked as she turned her gaze away from the signs.

"Who?" Sam questioned, silently singing the lyrics of "How Do Ya Like Me Now".

"Those people with the signs that say rodeos are bad," she answered, still in thought.

"Oh, right. The animal rights activists." Cat gave a sharp grin and continued. "Let's just say, and I'm not saying that everyone is like this—most of those organizations do a lot of good—that some of them are misinformed."

"And some of them are fanatics," Sam added. "But what they say has been true in the past. There were some things that people did at rodeos that really were cruel. Those practices have been stopped. Those people don't usually spend a lot of time at the back of the rodeo grounds and don't know quite how much pride owners take in animals like bucking bulls and bucking horses. And not many people know how little work those animals actually do. Chiquita works much harder than most of them."

"And there are always vets on hand in case, for example, a calf gets hurt when it's roped," Cat explained, leaning forward from the back of the truck to talk to her in the front seat.

"But as in every horse business, there are people who will be abusive and give the industry a bad name." Sam sighed. Alyson could tell he was more than just a little bit upset at his own explanation. "People like Tom and Josh who don't care about their animals give rodeo a bad name. But then, that's present at every stable everywhere."

Alyson nodded at the answer to her question. She didn't quite know what to say, and she didn't want to upset her friends any more than she feared she already had.

"All righty…we'll park and then get the horses ready." Sam broke her thoughts with words that sounded much more cheery than they needed to be.

He guided the trailer into a spot behind a small grandstand. It was a little more than two hours before the event was to begin, but the area was crowded with horses, trailers, and people. He parked in a spot that gave them a small shady area to themselves and shut off the engine.

They scrambled out of their seats, Alyson standing for a moment outside the truck to soak up a little bit of the atmosphere. There definitely was a buzz to the rodeo grounds she hadn't felt at any dressage trials. Everything at the trials had been so serious. Here the feeling was relaxed and fun, yet professional at the same time. She knew she couldn't explain the sensation if she tried.

A dirt-covered cowboy sauntered in front of them leading an enormous paint gelding, the number on his back hanging off by a thread and flapping in the wind. She could see that his face was set determinedly even though the hat shaded much of it.

Other competitors still had their number intact on their backs, like a very young man flipping a rope in his hand, a shining belt buckle adorning his middle. Women wearing tight jeans and revealing tops carried beers to a group of friends. Alyson's old friends would have joked if they'd seen this scene. Before, Alyson would also have laughed, but now she felt strangely a part of the surroundings. She *understood* the surroundings.

Alyson helped Cat and Sam get their horses ready while they waited for Lisa and Mark to arrive. Looking at Buck, who was especially handsome in his show-clean tack, Alyson thought of Tom and Josh. She wondered if they would be there tonight, but she decided against asking. There was no reason why they wouldn't be, and she didn't want to, once again, upset her friends.

"Boo!" Sam jumped gently at her from behind and wrapped his arms around her waist, rocking her into his grip.

Alyson started and fell back into him. She had been startled violently out of her thoughts but was happy for his embrace. "Sheesh, you scared me half to death." She mocked anger, but couldn't keep a straight face as she looked up at him.

"Come on, Cat's going to warm up the horses so that we can walk around a little bit. I'll show you what the rodeo's all about."

The rodeo grounds appeared much bigger than she figured they would be as Sam guided her through the people. Tack vendors, booksellers, and food stands crowded the area where they were walking, just in front of the main grandstand.

They neared a circular object that looked like an inflatable swimming pool. In the center was a plastic bull with a rope around the barrel. As they approached it, Alyson hesitated.

"Go on," Sam urged. "I'll pay for your ride," he said, reaching into his pocket to pull out a few coins.

"Oh, no. No way—I'll kill myself," she assured him.

"That's why it's done in that inflatable thing. If you fall off you won't get hurt," he reminded her, an evil grin spreading across his face. "Come on. You can do it."

Something about the way he encouraged her swept all doubt from her mind. Alyson climbed into the ring and mounted while Sam handed the money to the man controlling the ride.

The bull began to move. At first, it turned slowly and in one direction. Making sure she only held onto the rope with one hand and didn't touch anything with the other, Alyson rocked with the bull's movements.

With a jolt, it began to spin in the other direction and nearly unseated her. But she clung onto it even as the bull spun faster. After a few moments, it began to buck much higher than it had been before.

Hopelessly, Alyson gripped the rope and closed her legs tightly, but it was no use. She went flying, landing with a bounce against the ring's wall.

Clambering up onto her feet, she moved unsteadily by the wall. She climbed over and onto the stairs, tripping and tumbling into Sam.

Reacting quickly, he grabbed and steadied her until she could stand on her own.

Regaining her footing, Alyson apologized, "Sorry, I'm just a little dizzy."

"That's okay. It seems that I have a certain dizzying effect on girls." he joked, letting go of her arms when she was sure she was steady.

He was just quick enough to dodge her punch. "Shut up! You are such a jerk, you know that?"

"Why thank you." He beamed as though what she'd said had been a compliment.

They wandered around the grounds before returning to the trailer. Sam pointed out different things that she would have to know for the day she competed. All too soon, though, it was time for Sam to mount and meet Mark and Cat.

When they reached the trailer, Mark and Cat were sitting on Buck and Gabby, holding Poco's reins, as they talked with Brad.

"Hey guys," Brad greeted them as they approached. "How's it going?"

"Pretty good. We'll be competing tonight in penning. Mark and I rope tonight, Cat goes tomorrow, and Alyson barrel races on Saturday," Sam explained.

"Cat's been telling me about your little mare." Brad faced her. "She sounds cute. I'll be anxious to see how she runs."

"They're both really good." Mark winked at Alyson, who blushed at the compliment.

"Since you don't have your mare here tonight, did you want to ride Brooks? He's here but no one's competing on him. I just use him to calm my young horse in the trailer. That's the one I'll be riding," Brad offered, leaning against the trailer.

"Sure!" Alyson jumped at the chance to have a horse to ride around the grounds rather than trying to keep up with the others on foot.

They followed Brad, and Alyson saddled up Brooks. Once ready, Alyson guided the dun gelding into the warm up arena with her friends.

For a half an hour or so, they walked, trotted, and loped. Alyson practiced slide stops and spins, and even got a compliment from a woman who was watching her.

Happily, she even tried to rope again, although didn't come anywhere near the faux calf. She could hear snickers from behind her and didn't want to look back. She could guess who it was without turning her head. Out of the corner of her eye she recognized Josh's paint and Tom's striking bay.

Sam looked at her with concern. Alyson gathered the rope and handed it back to him with a shrug. "I don't care if they laugh at me. They'll stop smiling when they see how I compete on Saturday."

"They'll laugh at you for riding an Arab." He tossed his head in the direction of Mark, who was talking to Tom and Josh from atop Gabby. It was easy to tell they were making fun of the chestnut Arab.

"Not my problem." She gritted her teeth and continued to practice.

Within moments, it was time for Sam, Cat, and Mark to compete.

* * *

"Yeehaw! You are looking at the best team penners ever!" Sam grinned and practically lifted Alyson off of her feet, gripping her waist.

"So much for humility," Cat muttered, letting Buck's hoof go from her hand before she moved to the next foot, checking for rocks.

"I saw, anyway. You don't have to tell me you won. But hey, it's only one night. You still have Sunday before you actually win anything," Alyson loosened Brooks' cinch and made sure he was tied securely before leaving him.

"You guys are no fun." He secured the hay net on the side of the trailer so that Poco could eat while they relaxed before competing in roping, just an hour later.

"Why don't we go get something to eat?" Mark asked as he led Gabby to the other side of the trailer, where hay and water were waiting for the gelding.

"I'm starved," Cat said.

Alyson nodded her head in agreement. She hadn't eaten since breakfast that day, being far too nervous, but was now beginning to feel the hunger pangs in her stomach.

They left the horses, settled and comfortable, and wandered over to the vendors to buy something to eat. But as they were walking, Tom and Josh, looking very cocky with two huge rodeo belt buckles on their belts, stopped them in their tracks.

"Are you guys ready to lose?" Josh sneered. "I hear you guys showed up with two Arabs. That's just nuts. Arabs at a rodeo? You really weren't expecting to win anything, were you?"

Alyson couldn't believe what he'd just said. He was talking like some idiot from a bad movie, but he was actually serious. She wanted to say something in return, but Sam spoke up first, his voice bristling, "We'll see who's going to be the loser in an hour. And yes, we'll be competing with two Arabs, and what does that matter? But now, I want to enjoy myself. The only way I can do that is if you get out of my face. Get it?"

"Fine," Josh looked miffed. "In an hour we'll see who's the better roper."

* * *

Sam paced for the rest of the hour. They couldn't get him to even sit down with his food. He was as nervous as a cat in a kennel and there was no way to get him to calm down.

Alyson dragged him, when they had finished eating, to the gate on the backside of the arena to watch the professional team ropers. He looked at them with hawk-sharp eyes, studying every movement they made.

"Would you relax?" She gripped his arm and rubbed her fingers through his. They stood near the fence, peering through the top two bars.

"How can I? Everything is counting on this next round," he muttered, not meeting her gaze.

"Everything? What's counting on this? Bragging rights and nothing more. You can't let them overpower you like this."

"You don't understand. Tom and Josh aren't just friendly competition." He rotated between placing his left and right feet on the bottom bar of the fence.

"I know that. All I'm saying is that you began roping for fun, not just to beat these two guys who'll probably lose interest in rodeo by the time they're eighteen." She placed a comforting hand on his shoulder.

They were now both ignoring the roping in the arena, the roar of the crowd, and the sound of horses' hooves near them. Sam looked up.

"You know what? You are so right it's scary." He tossed her a grin and then straightened his stature, still leaning slightly on the fence.

"Why, how kind of you to notice," Alyson answered sarcastically.

From behind them, they could hear the clutter of hooves and the heavy, familiar breathing of two horses. They turned to see Mark, mounted on Gabby and holding Poco's reins. That night it was only the two guys competing. Cat would be roping the next evening.

"Hey," he called. "Let's go or you'll miss your round."

"Wish me luck," Sam told her, taking his horse and mounting in one easy swing.

"You've already got all of it. You've got to save some for me," she called with a grin.

The guys trotted off to warm up while Alyson watched the rest of the team roping. Cat joined her a few minutes later. They waited nervously while the rounds began, happy to see that no one had yet had much good luck. Two left without even touching the calves, one ran it too far and couldn't rope it, and one had clocked a time with a broken barrier.

Up next was Tom. He trotted across the arena, posting easily atop a different horse than he'd been riding the day they had visited the ranch the first time. This was a sturdy, definitely very tall, stallion. He was a plain dark brown, but he looked magnificent in the arena. His stallion characteristics, like the crest on his neck, only added to his beauty. It was easy to tell that he was highly bred to be a rodeo horse.

Tom positioned the bay stallion into the chute. The barrier was pulled taught across it. Since this arena was quite large, the calf would get much longer a head start than back at the ranch. He had to be careful not to let his horse go too soon.

He nodded. Within seconds, the calf was free and he and the stallion were rocketing across the dirt. Expertly, Tom swung two sharp turns with the rope and landed it around the calf's neck. Jumping off his stallion as the horse slid to a stop, Tom flipped the calf and tied his legs together. The calf remained on the ground for six seconds after he had remounted and let the rope slack. Tom clocked a blazing time of 14 seconds.

Two more long runs passed before it was Josh's turn. Josh, too, rode a different horse. This time it was a stocky bay snowflake Appaloosa mare. She trotted into the chute, muscles bulging from what looked like daily conditioning, tail and mane long and flowing.

They shot from the chute after the calf, and Josh determinedly roped and flipped it. The calf, one that hadn't been roped yet that day, struggled as hard as it could, but Josh managed to tie it. This one, too, stayed down. Josh had done it in 16 seconds.

Now Tom was in first and Josh was in third, just milliseconds behind the guy who'd gone before him. The top five finishers would go on to the final round, and there were only four more ropers left, Mark and Sam included.

Mark was up first of the four. Gabby looked magnificent as they floated across the arena, neck arched, mane and tail flying behind him, and chestnut coat gleaming. Alyson couldn't figure out why Arabs weren't that popular at rodeos; they were certainly beautiful. She could see, though, how they could be called stupid by their frequent spooks.

Gabby seemed nervous as they entered and stood in the chute, but didn't do anything he wasn't supposed to. Mark nodded. The calf was let out.

Hesitating slightly so as not to barge through the barrier, Gabby burst out after the calf. Within two swings, the rope was resting around the calf's neck and Gabby was sliding to a stop.

Mark raced to the calf, grabbed its legs with all the determination he had inside of him, and held them while he wrapped the piggin' string twice around with lightning speed. Filled with pride, he got up and remounted, letting the rope fall slack. Luckily, the calf didn't even try to struggle. Mark made an amazing time of 13 seconds.

Alyson could hear the cheer of the crowd as she hugged Cat tightly, the announcer crying out about the kid on the Arabian that had smoked every guy so far on a Quarter Horse.

Sam was the last one to rope, so they had to watch two more ropers before they were able to even see him in the arena. Mark returned to them, face aglow, patting Gabby as though the horse had just saved his life. He wanted to watch Sam's run, but there was not enough time to cool Gabby and come back, so Cat offered to take care of the gelding. She'd seen Sam rope so many times that missing him once wouldn't make a difference.

Mark hopped off gratefully and waited. They observed the two other riders nervously, although none clocked times close to Mark's. Alyson's stomach was churning by the time she caught sight of Poco at the far end of the arena.

Sam was flipping his rope in small circles as though he could do it in his sleep (and he probably could) while he moved Poco towards the chutes. Entering without wasting time, Sam positioned him. When they were ready, he nodded for the calf.

The clang of the calf's chute releasing could be heard as far as the other end of the arena; the noise of the crowd had died down to a low drone. Hastily, Sam shot Poco towards the calf. Alyson could see his attention was pinned nowhere but on the calf.

He flicked the rope around and tossed it. At first the rope looked as though it wouldn't land near the calf, but it twisted in the air and landed with perfect accuracy. Poco slid to a stop.

Sam jumped from the gelding's back and raced to the calf, half stumbling as he reached it. Thankfully, it didn't look as though he'd hesitated too much, for he had the calf tied within moments of the blunder.

A smile flitting across his face for an instant, Sam remounted and let the rope slack. The judges' flags waved to show that the six seconds were over and the calf was still down. He gave Poco an appreciative pat and watched for his time on the board.

After what seemed like forever, the time flashed on the scoreboard. The number 22.3 pounded into their minds for a moment before they realized what they actually saw. Sam had roped with the speed of a stampeding herd of wild horses, but he had broken the barrier.

A despondent look passing over his face, Sam moved Poco out of the arena. They had already begun to clear the arena for the next event.

Chapter 10

"I still can't believe I did that," Sam shoved his western saddle into the trailer's tack room, followed by Chiquita's bridle, and shut and locked the door.

"Would you go easy on yourself? You did fine. You roped like a pro even if you did break the barrier," Alyson said as she let Chiquita's hoof drop to the ground after cleaning it.

"But still..."

"You should be happy. Mark's in first place right now. That's really good. And you still have penning." She ran a hand over the mare's hindquarters, rubbing the top of her tail.

"I know. I just wanted to show Tom and Josh that we could beat them." Sam moved around Chiquita's hind end and unlatched the doors of the trailer.

"But you did. They were blown away by your time. I know it. And they practically fainted when they found out Mark was in first." This brought a smile to her lips. "Anyway, I don't want to hear one more word about roping until Cat's round begins tonight."

He grinned innocently and helped her load Chiquita into the trailer. Butterflies rampaged through her stomach, even though, once again, Alyson wouldn't be competing. That night, all they were going to do was cheer on Cat while she roped and get Chiquita used to the sights and sounds of the rodeo. She'd have to ride the next day.

"Incoming!" She heard from behind her.

Turning, Alyson spotted Buck, the lead rope slung over his back, sauntering towards them. His coat was shining with health and it showed that Cat groomed him daily. Smiling, she caught the gelding and guided him into the trailer.

"Think you'll survive another night of rodeo?" Mark pulled up alongside her as she stepped out of the trailer, latching the rope across the horses' behinds. Cat hurried to help them close the doors.

"I don't know yet. Ask me after tomorrow. By then it's likely I'll be dead," she told him with a sparkle in her eyes.

They piled into Sam's pick up and were off for yet another day of competition.

* * *

Chiquita tossed her head and rolled her eyes nervously, sidestepping around the backside of the rodeo grounds. She looked at every trailer and almost jumped from her skin at every noise. She was sweating after only a few minutes of walking around.

Trying to stay as calm as she could, Alyson rubbed her hand soothingly along the mare's neck. Chiquita snorted and tossed her head again. Out of nowhere, the crowd suddenly began to roar and loud music boomed. Chiquita swerved violently and jerked up her head in an attempt to get Alyson's grip to loosen on her mouth so she could run.

Barely in the saddle, Alyson regained her composure and set to calming the mare. Chiquita settled a little more with each revolution of the rodeo grounds. She was even content to graze some dry grass by the trailers. That was, of course, until Tom appeared in front of them.

"You had the nerve to show up on an Arab?" he laughed as though Mark and Gabby hadn't beaten him the day before.

"And you have the nerve to block my path?" She tried to steer the nervous mare around him, but Tom just sidestepped, obstructing her movement.

Chiquita, upset at Alyson's sudden feeling of annoyance and the constant changing of reins, flicked her head up and down again. Alyson could barely handle her while trying to listen to Tom's words.

The boy laughed. "Look at her, she's such a twerp you can't even get her to stand still."

Tom put his hand on the reins close to the bit and harshly pulled down to try and get Chiquita to stand still. Alyson knew this was his way of patronizingly trying to help her, but she didn't want *anyone* yanking on her horse's mouth.

"Let go of my horse!" she cried, pulling Chiquita back from him, hoping she hadn't been too harsh on the mare's mouth. She wanted to get away from Tom while trying not to further upset Chiquita at the same time.

Tom laughed again as the bay mare rolled her eyes and anxiously called out shrilly for the comfort of easygoing Buck. "You guys are such a lost cause. There's no way you're going to win anything barrel racing, and Mark won't win a thing roping. It's so pathetic it's sad."

"Aren't you the one who was beat by an Arab yesterday?"

"That was just luck. You just wait 'till Sunday. That's when we'll see who gets the buckle." At rodeos, she'd learned, the winners received belt buckles at the end of the competition.

Just as Alyson was about to bust—she was sick and tired of the twins' taunts—Sam jumped into the discussion.

"What's going on here?" he demanded, placing a soothing hand on Chiquita's sweaty neck. The mare immediately pricked her ears forward and sniffed him in hopes of receiving a treat.

"Just trying to get your girlfriend to wise up about competing on that horse."

"Well, we'd rather you didn't. This is supposed to be fun for all of us, so if you've nothing else to say we'll be getting on with our business." He suddenly seemed a lot taller than Tom, and he looked as though he could easily punch out the other guy's face.

"Fine," Tom grumbled and spun on his heel in the other direction.

"Come on." Sam ran his hand over Chiquita's neck and face, the mare breathing a heavy sigh. "Cat's competing in a couple of minutes. Let's get this girl cooled out and give her some hay."

* * *

Alyson, Sam, and Mark watched from the back arena gate as Buck's short tail flicked back and forth and he trotted around the arena. Cat posted determinedly in the saddle, flipping her rope in mechanical circles. She made competing look easy; not an ounce of her body seemed tense.

The buckskin Appaloosa gelding circled at a buoyant trot for a few seconds, until Cat slowed him with a touch of her reins. She checked her cinch and breast collar to make sure they fit correctly, piggin' string clamped between her teeth. They proceeded into the chute. Cat watched carefully as the calf was loaded into its chute, the string that operated the barrier falling around its neck.

After a few moments of absolutely no movement, Cat nodded sharply. The calf's chute's doors slammed open and the calf bolted straight and true. Cat kicked her heels into Buck's sides and they rushed off after it.

Buck's tail waved like a small flag in the wind as he galloped. Cat snapped the rope in three revolutions before finally tossing it. The rope looped perfectly around the calf's neck while Buck slid down on his hocks.

She jumped from his back and ran as fast as she could towards the calf. She grabbed it firmly and brought it to the ground, taking its front foot and letting the slip fall over it. With her other hand she brought two of its back legs, and, in a snap, she had all three legs tied together.

With a triumphant nod, Cat remounted Buck, moved him forward, and let the rope slack. She gave Buck a hearty pat and watched the judges for the six seconds, knowing that the calf would not move. It didn't.

As the crowd clapped her round, Cat watched the time flash on the board. 13.25. It had been an excellent round, good enough to get her into the finals.

That night, after they had come home and settled Buck and Chiquita, they had a celebration in the barn. Alyson only wished that she would do just as well the next day.

* * *

Alyson barely slept that night, and she woke up wired the next morning. By six o'clock in the morning, they were all at the barn and getting Chiquita ready. By the time they'd loaded her into the trailer and were off to the rodeo grounds, the mare's bay coat was gleaming.

The morning passed as Alyson paced idly with nervousness. Sam comforted her every few moments. She knew she would have backed out of the competition had he not been there. Sam tried to force her to share his lunch with him, but she refused.

By the early afternoon, she was mounted and setting Chiquita through her paces in the warm up arena. Within a half an hour, Sam was wishing her luck with a quick kiss and she needed to rush to the track; a racetrack bordered the large arena, and barrel racing was run on the track.

This fact made Alyson more nervous than she'd been before. The track didn't look very wide, and although there was enough room for all the barrels and for the horses to run, she had to wonder. What would happen if a horse fell? Would they go slamming right into the fence? She certainly hoped not.

Alyson was to run second in a group of six racers. Only three would go on to the finals since there were so few) that day, so she felt pretty good about her odds. But her stomach was churning to no end and she wanted to get her run over with.

She still had ten minutes to go, and all she could do was trot Chiquita around and try to shake off her nervousness. She didn't want to make the mare more nervous than she already was, and she wished that *she* didn't feel quite so anxious.

Alyson could well feel the stares of all the other cowgirls—they, at least, looked normal in a cowboy hat—as they observed Chiquita moving. One even made a face at her, lifting her nose in the air and doing an expert flying lead change on a striking dapple-gray Quarter Horse.

Before she knew it, it was her turn to run. She had seen a part of the first girl's round, and it had been good. Anxiously, she moved Chiquita further forward onto the track and kicked her into a gallop.

Laying her ears back flat against her head, the little bay mare flew out at the barrels. Her legs churning beneath her with power from her muscles, she only slowed as they reached the first barrel.

Not nervous anymore, but fully engrossed in the run, Alyson signaled for the lead change between the first and second barrels. With precision, Chiquita executed the change and they snapped around the second barrel.

Alyson scrubbed her hands along the mare's neck, pressing into her mane and telling her to go faster. They neared the third barrel, and she sat slightly taller, slowing so that they could go around it safely.

They spun quickly, although much to wide, around the last barrel. As they reached the straightaway, Alyson kicked Chiquita on and pressed her hands into her neck, letting the reins go loose so the mare could run. Chiquita kicked into another gear and raced across the finish line, Alyson able to release her grip on the mare's mane and to sit up.

They slowed as Alyson patted her triumphantly, the crowd cheering their round. She knew they had done well, despite the wide turn around the third barrel. Chiquita was fairly small and lightning fast she would be much more effective than a bulky horse trying to spin on those turns.

Suddenly the announcer cried in surprise, "It's official! The girl with the little bay Arab is in first place with an 18.24!"

Her face aglow, she walked Chiquita around the track to the backside of the grounds. They did it! Although only one other person had raced, she had beaten them when no one but her friends had thought she could. *Now* what would Tom and Josh have to say?

Sam practically pulled her off Chiquita, Cat taking the mare to cool her off, when they reached the track gate to the backside. He swept her into his arms and drew her into a long and passionate kiss. When they broke apart, he held her with a glow in his eyes. "You're a real cowgirl, Aly. No one's going to catch you today. You'd better be ready to run tomorrow."

They walked back to the trailer together, there happily greeted by the upbeat chords of the song "With Me", by Lonestar.

*   *   *

That night Alyson *did* sleep. She had crashed from the emotional high of the afternoon and the celebration they'd shared, once again, back at the barn. She hadn't seen Josh or Tom for the rest of the day, but she could see their spit-less expressions on their faces in her mind. Chiquita got an extra couple of carrots that night.

The next day, they left at the same time in the morning after Alyson had again thoroughly groomed Chiquita. Once at the rodeo grounds, she brought Chiquita out of the trailer, but did nothing more than tie her on the shady side of it with a bucket of water and a small flake of hay.

Sam, Cat, and Mark penned three calves in the morning, but they lost one close to the end and that left them nearly in last place. They were not altogether disappointed, though; they had made a good round but had made a slight mistake. They still had two roping rounds to go and Alyson had barrel racing to go.

Cat roped first, just before lunchtime. She brought Buck into the chute with determination on her face. They raced out of the chute after the calf, but it ran too far and she was unable to rope it. Disappointedly, she cooled Buck out and put him away with a flake of hay and water.

Just a few moments later, Mark began his round on Gabby.

"Good luck," Alyson wished him, the butterflies growing in her stomach. There was just an hour before she had to run her round. She was grateful for Sam's presence by her side as they watched.

That day, Mark posted nervously to the steady rhythm of Gabby's trot. The chestnut gelding seemed to pick up on this and his head was raised, his tail flowing free as he moved.

They pulled into the chute and Mark nodded for the calf. At what seemed like the same moment, Gabby and the calf shot from one end of the arena headed to the other.

Mark swung the rope four times before he landed it around the calf's neck. Gabby snapped to a stop as Mark sprung from his back. Expertly, he tied three legs and let the calf from his hands. It didn't stir, even as he remounted and even as the rope slacked. They had put in an excellent time: 13.55, which put them in first place for the time being.

After watching nervously as the rest of the contestants roped their calves, the results were in. Mark was the high school calf-roping champion of the rodeo on Gabby. Everyone in the audience cheered as they made their way around the arena in a victory lap, many people in surprise. A teenager riding a little chestnut Arabian gelding had just beat every other calf roper his age riding Quarter Horses at the rodeo that year.

* * *

Chiquita bobbed her head and sidestepped along the track, but Alyson sat still. In her mind she saw the three barrels and the path they would take around them. Deep nervousness fizzled through her body as she tried to remember everything her friends had told her.

Another horse zipped by them, and Chiquita wheeled around before moving forward on the track again.

"Easy, big girl," Alyson soothed, stroking the mare's sweaty neck.

It was hard to believe that she'd done the same course yesterday. She didn't know how she would manage to do it again, even though the previous day had seemed quite easy.

It was also incredibly hard to believe that she actually had a chance to win. She had to repeat to herself hundreds of times that she had finished in second place after all six rounds. And now it was all facing her. She could win and show everyone that an Arab, no, two Arabs, could win at one rodeo on the same day.

After many tense moments, Alyson was close enough to her turn to head down the track. Nervously she watched as the competitor before her began her run on a huge sorrel. She scanned the crowd nervously for her friends, but her eyes could not catch their images.

As soon as she could, Alyson sent Chiquita off at a gallop towards the first barrel. Chiquita laid her ears back and ran as though she were possessed. She seemed to know that this run counted much more than the other hand, and she wanted to win.

Alyson snapped her reins to the right, spinning Chiquita dangerously close to the barrel. The bay made a perfect turn even though it was very sharp.

They galloped on to the next one, Alyson's hands pressing on Chiquita's neck to urge her on. She signaled for the lead change and Chiquita responded instantly.

Alyson slowed her slightly in preparation for the turn. But just as she had guided Chiquita half way around, the mare faltered. She stumbled violently, and when she tried to regain her race to the other barrel, her feet slipped out from underneath her.

She gripped with her legs and tried to hold Chiquita's head up. But the mare's body pushed her to the ground. Alyson tumbled over her neck and onto the dirt.

For a few seconds, the world spun around as she rolled, the sky blending into the ground. In vain, she gripped the dirt, but she only kept rolling. Even when she stopped rolling, she couldn't tell the difference between air and ground.

Two familiar hands gripped her and stopped the world from twisting. At first, she felt that she knew the hands that held her, but her mind didn't register who it was.

"Aly, are you okay?" Cat's voice was recognizable now.

From in front of her, Cat asked again, "Are you okay? Can you hear me?"

Alyson blinked and her vision cleared. "Yeah, yeah…I'm fine. What about Chiquita?"

Cat's expression changed as she helped her to her feet. As she turned, wiping off her jeans, Alyson saw Chiquita.

Sam had one hand near her bit on the reins and other pressing on her shoulder. She was prancing around him, her inside leg lifted quickly every time it hit the ground. It was obvious even to Alyson that the leg had already started to swell. Mark was carefully pulling off the heavy western saddle that sat on her hot, sticky back.

"Easy." She could hear him say. "Easy, you're fine."

She quickly realized that Brad's trailer was backing up onto the track. She must have been out of it longer than she thought—long enough for him to get the trailer.

Sam turned Chiquita quickly so that she couldn't move away from him and tightened his grip on her reins. Brad tossed him a halter; the sudden movement spooked the mare, but Sam had such a hold on her mouth that she couldn't run away. Haștily, he managed to switch the bridle for the halter. Mark and Brad opened the back doors the van and Sam forced Chiquita into the trailer. He tied her in and closed the barrier before hopping out.

"No!" Alyson cried, and she tried to reach Chiquita, but Cat's hands held her back firmly.

"Wait—she's going to go to the vet and…"

But she didn't hear the rest of what Cat said. With blind rage, she pushed Cat harshly away and rushed up to where the doors of the van were already closing behind Chiquita.

"No!" she cried again as Sam caught her and held her back.

"Shh, shh…" he soothed her as he dragged her off the track and back to the trailer.

Even as they reached the trailer, he gripped her as though she were about to run away, although she was too numb to struggle anymore.

"When you fell," he started, forcing her to sit in the cab of the truck for a moment and wrapping up his hands in hers. "When you fell, she hurt her leg very badly. She was dead lame when she got up but she tried to keep running. We stopped her in time to get her into the trailer. Brad's taking her to the vet."

The words seemed to pass right through her as she sat in the truck. She pulled on her seat belt mechanically as Sam jumped into the driver's seat and started the engine. As the truck came to life, so did the chorus of Trisha Yearwood's song "I Would Have Loved You Anyway". But she didn't hear it.

It seemed to take ten years to drive through town to the local large animal vet. They seemed to hit every red light in town—and there weren't many to begin with.

When they reached the small parking lot, they jumped from the truck and met Cat, who had driven herself and Mark in her parent's car. Brad had arrived just a few minutes earlier.

Sam and Cat rushed around the back of the building to help the vet and Brad with the trailer doors and handling the frantic mare. Mark and Alyson seemed to lag behind near the front doors.

"It'll be okay," Mark assured her, holding open the entrance door to let her go in first. "You'll see. It'll all be fine."

"I don't know. I just don't know. It was all so sudden." She sat down in a chair next to him in the vet's foyer. They were alone in the room, which was almost soothing.

"I really hate to sound cheesy, but there's something I have to say." Mark turned sideways in the seat so that he could face her, although she only stared straight ahead.

"Go ahead." Alyson nodded, sniffing and wiping tears from her face.

"Do you remember that afternoon that you first met Lisa and Gabby, and Sam and I were teaching you about roping? Do you remember what I told you?"

"Sure, I remember the day but I don't remember what you said. What does that have to do with this?" She tried not to sound desperate and rude, but she feared the words came off sounding that way.

"Well, I told you about remounting and letting the rope loose and how the calf has to stay tied for six seconds. And I told you that it's the worst feeling in the world waiting to see if your wrap's going to hold or not. You can never be sure how it's going to turn out.

"It kind of seems like now, you know. The rope's gone loose and there's no telling what's going to happen. It'll be terrible and it could come out for better or worse, but there's always that chance that your tie will hold, especially when you give an extra wrap and a half hitch."

Alyson looked up at him, her eyes blurred with tears. "Six second slack, right?"

Mark nodded, placing a hand on her arm to comfort her.

About the Author

Rachel Hector was born in 1986 in St. Louis, MO, but has lived in California most of her life. She's very involved in the world of horses and is especially interested in the sport of rodeo and now lives in the rodeo town of Salinas. She will attend university, where she will study veterinary medicine or history, another love of hers.

0-595-21513-0

Printed in the United States
4086

9 780595 215133